A Treasury of
FAIRY TALES

A Treasury of
FAIRY TALES

With Classic Illustrations
Edited by Michael Foss
Designed by Martin Bristow

MICHAEL O'MARA BOOKS LIMITED

First published in Great Britain by
Michael O'Mara Books Limited
20 Queen Anne Street
London W1N 9FB

Picture research Lesley O'Mara

ISBN: 0 948397 30 6

Printed in Spain by Graficas Estella, Navarra

Contents

Contents

The 3 Bears take
a Morning Walk.

R Andre

Goldilocks and the Three Bears

ONCE upon a time there were Three Bears who lived together in a house in a wood. One was a Small Wee Bear, and one was a Middle-sized Bear, and the other was a Great Huge Bear.

They each had a bowl for their porridge. There was a little bowl for the Small Wee Bear, and a middle-sized bowl for the Middle Bear, and a great bowl for the Great Huge Bear. And they had three chairs and three beds, little ones for the Small Wee Bear, middle-sized ones for the Middle Bear, and great big ones for the Great Huge Bear.

One day before breakfast, while they were waiting for their porridge to cool, they took a walk in the wood. And while they were away, young Goldilocks came to the house. First she looked in the window, then she peeped through the keyhole, and seeing nobody was at home she lifted the latch. She went in and saw the bowls of porridge steaming on the table.

Now, if Goldilocks had been a good girl, she would have waited for the Bears to come home, and perhaps they would have asked her to breakfast. For they were good Bears – a little rough as many Bears are – but kind and friendly. But Goldilocks was a naughty girl, and she began to help herself.

So first she tasted the porridge of the Great Huge Bear, and that was too hot. She didn't like that. Then she tasted the porridge of the Middle Bear, and that was too cold. She didn't like that. And then she tasted the porridge of the Small Wee Bear, and that was just right. So she ate it all up.

Then Goldilocks sat down in the chair of the Great Huge Bear, and that was too hard. Then she sat in the chair of the Middle Bear, and that was too soft. And then she sat in the chair of the Small Wee Bear, and that was just right. So she sat there until the bottom came out of the chair and she went plump upon the ground. And then Goldilocks said a wicked word.

Then Goldilocks went upstairs into the bedroom. First she lay on the bed of the Great Huge Bear, but that was too high. Then she lay on the bed of the Middle Bear, but that was too low. And then she lay on the bed of the Small Wee Bear, and that was just right. So she pulled the bed-clothes up to her chin, and went fast asleep.

After a while, the Three Bears came home, as they expected the porridge to be cool by now. But when they looked at the table, they saw a spoon standing in each bowl of porridge.

'SOMEBODY HAS BEEN AT MY PORRIDGE!'
said the Great Huge Bear in his loud, gruff voice.

And the Middle Bear saw the spoon in his bowl.

'Somebody has been at my porridge!'
said the Middle Bear in his middle-sized voice.

Then the Small Wee Bear saw the spoon in his bowl, and all his porridge was gone.

'Somebody has been at my porridge, and has eaten it all up!'
said the Small Wee Bear in his little, sharp voice.

When they found that their breakfast was disturbed , the Three Bears began to look around the house. The Great Huge Bear noticed that the cushion was not straight in his big, hard chair.

'SOMEBODY HAS BEEN SITTING IN MY CHAIR!'
said the Great Huge Bear in his loud, gruff voice.

And the Middle Bear saw a dent in the soft cushion of his chair.

'Somebody has been sitting in my chair!'
said the Middle Bear in his middle-sized voice.

And you know what Goldilocks had done to the third chair.

'Somebody has been sitting in my chair, and has broken
the bottom out of it!'
said the Small Wee Bear in his little, sharp voice.

Then the Three Bears went upstairs to look in the bedroom. The Great Huge Bear saw the pillow out of place on his bed.

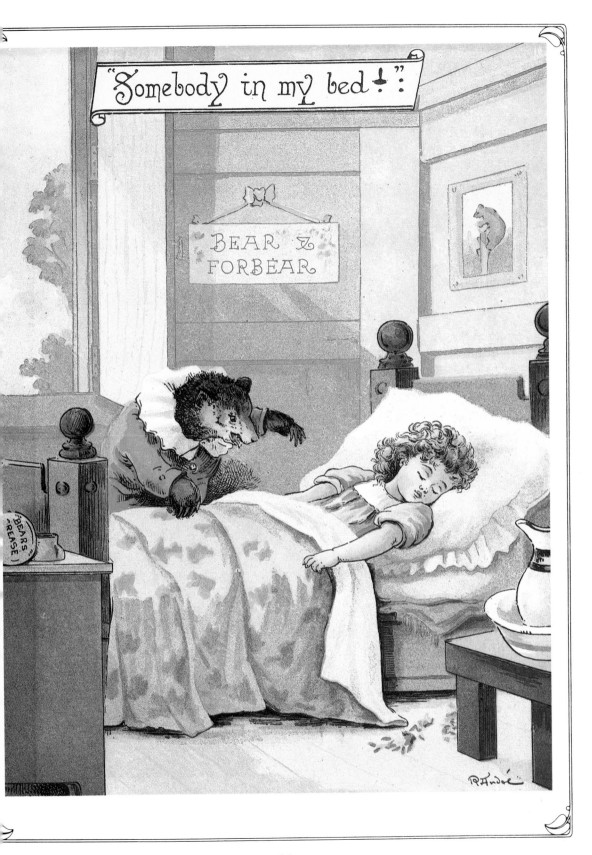

'SOMEBODY HAS BEEN LYING IN MY BED!'
said the Great Huge Bear in his loud, gruff voice.

And the Middle Bear saw that his bedspread was out of place.

'Somebody has been lying in my bed!'
said the Middle Bear in his middle-sized voice.

And when the Small Wee Bear looked at his bed, he saw a head of golden hair lying on his pillow, and that was definitely out of place.

'Somebody has been lying in my bed – and here she is!'
said the Small Wee Bear in his little, sharp voice.

In her sleep, Goldilocks heard the loud, gruff voice of the Great Huge Bear. But it seemed like the roar of the wind, or the rumble of thunder. And she heard the middle-sized voice of the Middle Bear. But it seemed like someone speaking in a dream. But when she heard the little, sharp voice of the Small Wee Bear, it was so sharp and shrill that she woke up at once.

Up she jumped. And when she saw the Three Bears on one side of the bed, looking very cross and bothered, she tumbled out of the other side and ran to the window. Now the Three Bears were good, tidy, healthy Bears, and they always opened their window in the morning. So Goldilocks leaped out of the window.

Perhaps she broke her neck in the fall. Or perhaps she ran into the wood and was lost. Or perhaps a policeman found her and took her away to the police station.

But the Three Bears never saw anything more of her.

'What great teeth you've got, Granny.'

Little Red Riding-hood

THERE was once a little country girl, a pretty little mite, who was the apple of her mother's eye. And her grandmother loved her even more than that, if possible. The fond old lady made the child a cloak and a hood out of red cloth. And in this the little girl looked as bright and as smart as a new penny, so that everyone called her Little Red Riding-hood.

One day, her mother made some custard pies and said to her daughter:

'Go and see how Granny is, for I fear she's not very well. Take her this pie, and give her a kiss, and tell her to get better quickly.'

So Little Red Riding-hood set out at once, and as she was going through the wood to her Granny's house she met Mr. Wolf who had a good mind to eat her up right then and there. But he did not dare to, just at that moment, because some men were cutting trees nearby.

The Wolf fell in with the girl, whistling in a carefree way, and as they walked along he asked her, very politely, where she was going.

Now the poor child did not know how dangerous it is to talk to a Wolf, so she answered:

'I'm going to my Granny, to take her a custard pie and this little pot of butter from my Mamma.'

'Oh,' said the Wolf, as casual as you please, 'and does she live far away?'

'Not at all,' replied Little Red Riding-hood. 'Just at the other side of the mill, in the first house at the edge of the village.'

'Well,' said the Wolf, 'let's both go and see her. I'll go this way, and you go that, and we'll see who gets there first.'

Mr. Wolf began to run as fast as he could along the shortest way. But the little girl went the long way round, through the pretty places, where she could see the butterflies and gather a little bunch of flowers. So the Wolf arrived first at Granny's door.

Knock, knock, he went, and a voice answered: 'Who's there?'

'It's Little Red Riding-hood,' the Wolf replied in a small, squeaky voice, 'and I've brought you a custard pie and a pot of butter from my Mamma.'

Granny was in bed and not very well, so she cried: 'Pull up the latch and come in.'

The Wolf pulled up the latch and came in, and then he jumped upon the old lady and gobbled her up in a wink, for he had eaten

'What great eyes you've got, Granny.'

nothing in three days. Then he shut the door, and dressed himself in Granny's nightie, got into bed and waited.

After a while, Little Red Riding-hood arrived. She rapped on the door, knock, knock.

'Who's there?' answered a large, gruff voice.

When she heard this, the child was afraid. But then she thought that Granny had a cold, which had made her voice grow rather hoarse. So she answered:

'It's Little Red Riding-hood, with a custard pie and a pot of butter from Mamma.'

'I am ill, my dear,' said the Wolf, making his voice as soft as possible, 'so pull up the latch and come in.'

When the child entered, she saw a figure in the bed with a night-cap on and the bed-clothes pulled up to the eyebrows.

'Put the food on the table,' said the voice, 'and come into bed with your Granny.'

Little Red Riding-hood undressed and got into bed. She was astonished to find how strange her Granny had become.

'What great arms you've got, Granny,' she said.

'All the better to hug you, child!'

'What great legs you've got, Granny.'

'All the better to run, child!'

'What great ears you've got, Granny.'

'All the better to hear you, child!'

'What great eyes you've got, Granny.'

'All the better to see you, child!'

'And what great teeth you've got, Granny.'

'All the better to eat you up!'

And saying this, the wicked Wolf leapt on Little Red Riding-hood and ate her all up.

Rosa C. Petherick.

Puss in Boots

THERE was once a miller who had little to give to his three sons. He was very poor and when he died all that remained were his mill, his donkey, and his cat. So without sending for any lawyers, who would have swallowed everything, the sons shared what was left. The eldest son took the mill, the second the donkey, and the youngest had nothing but the cat.

The third son was not very pleased with what he had got.

'My brothers,' he said to himself, 'have done well. If they get together, they can make a living, with a mill and a donkey. But all I can do is eat my cat, make a muff of his skin, and then die of hunger.'

The cat, who had heard all this, put on a serious face and tried to comfort his master.

'Good master, do not worry,' said the cat. 'Just give me a bag and a pair of boots, so that I can scamper through the woods, and I will show you that you are better off than you think.'

Now the youngest son had seen the cat do many clever tricks to catch rats and mice. And he noted that the cat was very cunning. So he thought he would see what the cat could do.

When the cat was dressed very gallantly in a large pair of boots, and with a bag around his neck, Mr Pussy set out to try his luck. First, he hid himself in a rabbit warren and soon tricked a silly young bunny into his bag. Then off he went to the King's palace. And when the courtiers asked him what he wanted, he said he was

Mr Pussy set out to try his luck.

the servant of 'my lord, the Marquis of Carabas' (which was the title he gave to the miller's son), and that he had a present from his master for the King. And when he saw that the King was pleased with the rabbit, the cat caught other small animals, like hares and partridges, and gave them to the King, pretending that they all came from the Marquis of Carabas. The King began to feel very friendly towards this strange nobleman.

Now one day the cat heard that the King and his daughter, the most beautiful Princess in the world, were going to take a drive by the riverside. So Pussy went to his master and said:

'You are in luck today. Just go and wash yourself in the river at such and such a place, and leave the rest to me.'

While the miller's son was washing, the King passed by, and the cat began to shout:

'Help, help! My lord, the Marquis of Carabas is drowning!'

The King put his head out of the coach, and seeing it was the cat who brought him gifts that called, ordered the royal guards to save the good Marquis of Carabas.

As they were dragging the miller's son from the river, Mr Pussy, who had hidden his master's clothes, explained to the King that a band of robbers had stripped the Marquis and thrown him naked into the river. The King was very sorry to hear it, and at once offered the young man the finest clothes from his own wardrobe. And when the miller's son was dressed in these rich clothes, he looked every inch a Marquis, and the Princess looked on him tenderly and fell in love.

As soon as the miller's son was dressed and ready, he got into the coach and began to ride slowly back to the palace with the King and the Princess. The cat hurried on in front, and when he saw some mowers working in the fields, he called to them and said:

'Good people, if the King asks you, tell him this meadow belongs to the Marquis of Carabas. Do this, or I'll have you chopped as small as herbs for the pot.'

The mowers were so frightened by the cat's fierce face that they did as they were told. And the cat, hurrying on before, ordered the reapers and the ploughmen and the woodcutters to do the same. The King was amazed by the great lands owned by this Marquis.

Now the lands they were passing through really belonged to a

The cat became a most important person in the court.

rich Ogre who lived in a castle nearby. The cat, who knew all about the Ogre, called at the castle door and said, very politely, that he had heard many things but he could hardly believe that the Ogre had such wonderful magic powers.

'Can you, for example,' said the cat, 'turn yourself into an elephant, or a lion?'

'Easy,' said the Ogre. And the next moment, there was a lion on the floor of the castle, roaring and growling. The cat was so frightened he climbed up the gutter and took to the roof, stumbling about in his great boots that were not made for walking on the tiles.

After a while, the Ogre changed back into his own form, and the cat came panting down from the roof.

'Well,' said cunning Mr Pussy, 'that was very fine. But a large animal is one thing and small one another. Now, to change into a mouse, I should think that's impossible.'

'Impossible!' cried the Ogre. 'Why, it's the simplest thing in the world.'

And in the blink of an eye, there was a mouse scampering about the floor. With a leap, the cat pounced on the mouse, and gobbled it all up.

Meanwhile, the coach with the King and the Princess and the miller's son came by the castle, and the King decided to pay a visit. Surely some great lord must be the owner of such a grand castle. The coach rolled up to the castle door, and waiting there was the cat.

'Your Majesty is welcome,' he said, sweeping off his hat and bowing low. 'Welcome to the castle of my lord, the Marquis of Carabas.'

'What,' cried the King, turning to the miller's son, 'is this yours as well? Not only the lands and fields and woods, but this wonderful building also? Well, my lord, let us go in.'

The miller's son gave his hand to the Princess, and they went in after the King. And inside, they found waiting for them a great feast, which the Ogre had been preparing for his friends, before the cat brought his life to a sudden end.

Now the King was quite charmed with the fine things that belonged to the Marquis of Carabas, and the Princess was more and more in love with the handsome young man each moment. And when the King had drunk five or six glasses of wine, he turned to the miller's son and said:

'My Lord Marquis, if you don't become my son-in-law it will be your own fault, because you can see that my daughter is only too happy to marry you.'

So the miller's youngest son, who had set out from home with nothing but his father's cat, bowed low and married the Princess that same day.

And the cat became a most important person in the court, and never had to run after mice any more, except for fun.

Tom Thumb

A POOR woodcutter and his wife were lonely because they had no children.

'How nice it would be,' said the husband, puffing on his pipe, 'if we had children to play around us. The house is so quiet.'

'Yes,' sighed his wife, 'how happy I would be to have just one. Even if it were no bigger than my thumb, I'd love it dearly.'

Now strange though it may seem, the wife's wish was granted. Soon afterwards she had a baby boy, quite strong and healthy, but no larger than her thumb. So they called him Tom Thumb.

They gave the little fellow plenty of food, but he never grew any bigger. But in every other way he was a sharp, clever little lad, able to hold his own in the world of huge people and things all around him.

One day, the woodcutter was going out to work, but the cart was not ready.

'You go on, father,' said Tom. 'I'll look after the cart.'

'How can that be?' laughed his father. 'You can't reach over the horse's hoof.'

'Never mind,' said Tom. 'If my mother will harness the horse, I'll get in his ear and give him his orders.'

So Tom cried 'Go on' and 'Stop' and 'Left' and 'Right', and the horse trotted along as if by himself. Then the horse began to run faster, and as Tom was calling 'Gently, gently!', two strangers came by.

'That's odd,' said one, 'there's a cart going down the road, and I hear a carter talking, but I can't see anyone.'

'Yes, it is queer,' said the other, 'let's follow and see where it goes.'

The cart got to the wood safe enough, and the woodcutter took his tiny son out of the horse's ear and set him down, as lively as a cricket.

'Now there's a wonderful thing,' said one of the strangers who had been following. 'If we could get our hands on that little imp, we would make a fortune, showing him from town to town.'

So they went up to Tom's father and offered to buy the little fellow. But the woodcutter would not hear of it. What, sell his own flesh and blood! Then Tom, who had been listening, crept up his father's coat and whispered in his ear:

'Take the money, father, and let them have me. I'll soon come back to you.'

The deal was done for a large piece of gold, and away Tom went, perched on the brim of his new master's hat. But that evening, as they rested by the road, Tom ran into a ploughed field and slipped down an old mouse-hole.

'Good night, my masters,' he called, 'I'm off. You'll have to be sharp to look after me next time.'

When the strangers had gone, unable to find Tom, the little man came out of the mousehole and crawled into a large snail-shell to sleep. As he was settling down, he heard two robbers come by, and they were wondering how they could rob the parson's house.

'I'll tell you,' said a tiny voice from the ground.

'Who's there?' cried a thief, in a frightened whisper.

'Look down here, you blockhead,' said Tom. And when the robbers did, and found him, Tom told them that he could creep between the bars on the window, take the parson's money and throw it out of the window.

So Tom went along with the robbers and slipped through the bars into the parson's house. When he was inside, he bellowed:

'Do you want everything?'

'Softly, softly,' said the thieves outside, shaking in their shoes. 'You'll wake the house.'

'Very well,' shouted Tom, even louder than before. 'Hold out your hands. Here it comes!'

Well, this noise woke the cook, who sprang out of bed, and the robbers ran away as if there was a wolf at their heels. Then Tom slipped off to the barn before the cook could return, and settled down for the night in the hayloft.

In the morning, the cook got up at day-break to feed the cows, and going to the hayloft, she carried away a bundle of hay with Tom still in it, fast asleep. When he awoke, he was surprised to find himself, with some hay, in the mouth of a cow. The cow began to grind the hay and Tom had to dodge about to keep from being crushed. Then the cow gulped, and Tom found himself in the cow's stomach.

'It's rather dark in here,' he said. 'They forgot to put windows to let the sun in. A candle would certainly help.'

He did not care for his dark lodgings, which were in any case getting full up with hay.

'That's enough now,' he cried out as loud as he could. 'Don't bring me any more hay!'

The maid had just begun to milk that cow, and hearing someone speak but being unable to see anyone, she fell off the stool. Then she ran to fetch her master, the parson.

'Sir, sir, the cow is talking!' she cried.

'Woman,' replied the parson severely, 'you are surely mad.'

But when the parson went to see the cow, Tom was still shouting: 'Don't bring me any more hay!'

This frightened the parson too, and thinking that the animal was bewitched, he ordered it to be killed at once. When this was done, the cow was cut up, and the stomach, with Tom still in it, was thrown on the dunghill.

Now Tom began to struggle out of the stomach, and he had just got his head clear when a wolf came by and gobbled it all up, including little Tom Thumb. Tom wondered what to do and thought he had better have a chat with the wolf.

WARWICK GOBLE.

'Hold on, my friend,' Tom called out, 'I think I can show you a good treat.'

Then he told the wolf if he went to a certain house, which was really the house of Tom's father, he could creep through the drain and into the pantry, and there he would find ham, beef, cold chicken, roast pig, apple dumplings, cakes, and everything else his heart could wish.

The wolf didn't wait to be told twice. That very night, he crawled through the drain into the pantry, and ate and drank as much as he could hold. But he had eaten so much, he could not get back through the drain. At this moment, Tom began to bang and shout from inside the wolf.

'Easy down there,' said the wolf, 'if you make that row, you'll waken the house.'

'What's that to me?' cried the little fellow. 'You've had your fun, and now I'll make merry myself.'

And he shouted and sang until the woodcutter and his wife, awakened by the noise, peeped round the edge of the pantry door.

When he saw the wolf, the woodcutter was terrified. So he ran for his axe and gave his wife a scythe. He would strike the beast and then she would rip it open. But Tom Thumb heard them, and called out:

'Father, father, it's me in here. The wolf has swallowed me.'

Then the father gave the wolf a blow on the head with the axe, and killed him on the spot. Very carefully, they cut open the body, and out popped young Tommy, still bright and cheerful.

'Ah,' cried his mother, 'what fears we have had for you,'

'Yes,' said Tom, 'since we parted I think I've seen the world. And now I'm glad to come home and get some fresh air, for I've been rather too long in some cramped, dark places.'

'Well,' said his father, 'you are back now, and we will not sell you again for all the riches in the world.'

Then they all hugged and kissed, and his mother made him a great feast, and his father got him some clean clothes. After that, Tom Thumb stayed at home, in peace, with his father and mother. For although he had travelled and had many adventures, which he was pleased to tell you about, he agreed after all that there was no place like home.

The Emperor's
New Clothes

MANY years ago there was an Emperor who was so fond of clothes that he spent all his money on them. He cared for nothing else, and had a costume for every hour of the day. Instead of saying, as one usually did about an Emperor, 'Oh, he's in his council chamber,' the people in this country said, 'The Emperor is in his dressing room.'

One day, two swindlers came to the city and said they were weavers, able to make the most beautiful material you could imagine. The colours and the patterns were marvellous, but the cloth was even more wonderful than that. Only intelligent and virtuous people could see it. It was invisible to those who were dull, idle or worthless.

'That must be splendid stuff,' thought the Emperor. 'I'll be able to tell the wise men from the fools. Yes, I certainly must have some of that.'

So he paid the swindlers a lot of money, and they began work at once.

The swindlers bought the finest silk and the purest gold thread, which they locked away in a bag. Then they set up their looms and pretended to weave, passing the shuttles through the empty air far into the night. They seemed to be extremely busy.

The Emperor was very curious to see how they were getting on, but what if he saw nothing? By now, everyone in town knew the magical quality of the cloth, that it was invisible to fools.

The good old minister stared at the empty loom.

'No,' thought the Emperor, 'I'll send my old minister. He's a wise, loyal servant and he will not be fooled.'

So the good old minister went and stared at the empty loom. 'Good lord,' he thought, 'I can't see a thing.' But he took care not to say so. The swindlers begged him to step a little nearer, to look at this pattern and that colouring. And the poor old man stared as hard as he could, but saw nothing. Because, of course, there was nothing to see.

'Heavens,' he thought, 'is it possible that I'm a fool? Perhaps I am not fit for my position? I must keep this quiet. It will never do to say I can't see the cloth!'

So the minister told the Emperor that the material was truly wonderful, and the Emperor paid the swindlers yet more money, and the swindlers busily threw the shuttles across the empty looms. Then the Emperor sent another faithful servant to check the cloth, and he, not wanting to be a fool either, also noted the bold patterns and brilliant colours. Everyone in town was talking about this amazing stuff.

Then the Emperor thought he would take a look himself, and set out with the most important members of his court. The weavers were bent over their looms, working away at a breathless pace. At once, the courtiers stood behind the looms, pointing to the wonders of the design. What style! What imagination! What colours!

'But this is terrible!' thought the Emperor. 'I can see nothing at all. Am I a fool? Unfit to be Emperor? Oh, no, nothing could be worse than that!'

So he quickly said: 'Yes, it's beautiful. Nothing could be finer.' And he nodded with satisfaction at the empty frames.

'Beautiful!' said all the court, gazing hard and seeing nothing. Magnificent! Gorgeous! Fantastic! The word went round, from mouth to mouth, throughout the city, and everyone was delighted. The Emperor gave the swindlers more money, a decoration to wear in their button-holes, and the title of 'Gentlemen Weavers to His Majesty'.

Now the Emperor was to wear his new suit of this wonderful cloth in a special procession, and the swindlers stayed up all night, burning sixteen candles, to get it ready. With a flourish, they took the invisible stuff from the loom, cut the air with a huge pair of

He walked on naked.

scissors, and stitched away with needles without thread. At last, they cried:

'The Emperor's new clothes are ready!'

In the morning, the Emperor went to be dressed. The swindlers pretended to hold up the clothes, pointing out all the details. This was the trousers, this the coat, this the cloak, and so on.

'Everything is as light as a spider's web,' they explained. 'One might think you had nothing on, but that's the very beauty of it!' And everyone smiled and agreed.

Slowly, the Emperor took off all his clothes, and the swindlers pretended to give him one new piece after another. They pulled and fastened and tucked and smoothed, then they led the Emperor to the mirror and turned him round and round.

'How well His Majesty looks in his new clothes,' cried all the on-lookers of the court.

'Yes, don't they fit well?' said the Emperor. 'Now I'm quite ready.'

The servants who had to carry the end of the long cloak stooped and pretended to lift it from the ground, and walked solemnly with their hands in the air. The Emperor took his place under the canopy, the courtiers followed behind, and the procession began. The people were crowding the streets and hanging out of the windows.

'How beautiful the new clothes are,' they cried. 'What a design! What magnificent material! What a wonderful fit!'

They were the most successful clothes the Emperor had ever had.

But suddenly the voice of a little child sounded from out of the crowd:

'But he's got nothing on!'

And the people nearby began to whisper to each other:

'Did you hear what the child said? He's got nothing on. The Emperor has nothing on.'

And then the whole crowd was crying out:

'The Emperor has nothing on!'

The Emperor blushed terribly, for he knew it was true. But the procession must go on. He straightened his back and put on a stern face. His servants held up his invisible cloak, and he walked on naked.

Cinderella was dressed in tatters.

Cinderella

THERE was once a gentleman, a widower, who married for the second time. But this time his wife was the silliest, proudest woman in the whole land. She already had two daughters by a former husband, and they were every bit as foolish as their mother. But the gentleman also had a young daughter by his first wife, and she was as sweet a girl as you could find anywhere.

Now, the new wife could not bear this pretty, kind girl, because she made her own daughters look so grumpy and plain. So she gave her step-daughter the hardest and meanest work in the house. The two ugly young madams had the softest beds, the finest clothes, the best food – and they did no work. But the poor little step-daughter was like a slave in the house from morning to night. She slept on a straw mat in the attic. She had to wear old clothes that did not fit her. And when her work was done, she was told to go to the chimney-corner and sit among the cinders. For this reason she was called Cinderella.

But although Cinderella was dressed in tatters, with a face all grimy from work, she was still a hundred times kinder and prettier than the two lumpy step-sisters.

That year, the King's son gave a ball, and invited all the important people in the land. The two ugly sisters were invited. Since they were idle and rich, with expensive tastes, they had become well-known in the city. And at once they were in a dither about what to wear and how to look.

'I'll wear my red velvet, with trimmings of French lace,' said the eldest.

'I'll have to make do with my old petticoat,' sighed the younger. 'But I'll have my cloak with gold flowers and my diamond brooch. Of course, Cinderella must help us get ready.'

Cinderella worked willingly for her step-sisters, ironing and sewing and polishing. But it was not easy to make something attractive out of two ugly faces and two shapeless bodies.

'What a pity you're not going to the ball!' said the elder sister unkindly, as Cinderella was combing her tangled mop of hair.

'Oh, don't make fun of me,' cried the poor girl. 'How could I go in my rags?'

'Yes,' sneered the younger one, as Cinderella was trying to stuff her into a dress that was much too tight, 'people would laugh to see a Cinderella at a ball!'

At last, the sisters were in some sort of order, very richly dressed, though they still looked rather frightful. As they set off for the royal court, Cinderella watched them go with tears in her eyes.

As she sat weeping, suddenly her Fairy Godmother appeared and wanted to know what all the fuss was about.

Suddenly her Fairy Godmother appeared

'If only,' Cinderella whispered through her tears, 'if only I too could go to the ball.'

'And so you shall,' said the Godmother briskly. 'Just dry your eyes, child, and I'll arrange it.'

First, she sent Cinderella to the garden for a pumpkin. When she had brought the largest she could find, her Godmother touched it with her wand and in a moment it became the finest coach you ever saw, gilded all over with gold. Then Cinderella was told to look in the mouse-trap, where there were six plump mice, all alive. The Godmother gave each a tap of the wand and turned them into six dapple-grey horses. Next, Cinderella went back to the garden where she found, behind the watering-can, six lively lizards, which her Godmother turned into six footmen, stiff and proud in silver-buttoned coats.

The last person needed was a coachman. Cinderella hunted around until she found a large rat with a grand set of whiskers. The Godmother gave it a touch and it became a fat, jolly coachman with a red beard and an even redder nose.

'Well, child,' said the Fairy Godmother, 'how about that? Aren't you pleased with your horses and your carriage?'

'Oh yes, I am,' Cinderella replied. 'But how, Godmother dear, can I go to the ball in these old clothes?'

At once, her Godmother waved her wand and the dirty old clothes changed into the most beautiful ball dress. And around her neck was a string of pearls, and at her ears winked diamond earrings. Then, to complete the pretty picture, she found on her feet the daintiest little glass slippers in the world.

'Now, away you go and enjoy yourself,' said the Fairy God-mother. 'But remember, you must not stay one second beyond midnight, or all your fine things will change back to a pumpkin and little animals and rags.'

When Cinderella arrived at the palace, and came shyly into the ballroom, the Prince noted her at once and sent one of his courtiers to meet her. There was a sudden hush in the great hall, the dancers were still, the musicians stopped playing. Everyone was amazed at the beauty of the unknown lady. Then the Prince came and took Cinderella in his arms, and the music started, and they danced and danced, for the Prince could not take his eyes off her.

'You shall go to the ball,' said the Fairy Godmother.

After the dancing, all the court and all the guests went to eat. The Prince would touch nothing himself until he had waited on Cinderella, and he chose her the finest food and drink with his own hands. But Cinderella saw her two step-sisters, as plain as buckets, sitting hot and forgotten in a far part of the room. So she went to sit by them, and took them fruit that the Prince himself had given her. The sisters were very surprised, for they did not recognize this beautiful and graceful lady.

Then the dancing began again, and the Prince and Cinderella were so happy together, and so caught up in the music, that time just raced by. Suddenly the clock started to strike twelve. With a thump of her heart, Cinderella remembered the warning of her Fairy Godmother. With a little cry she fled from the ballroom.

As she ran, she lost one of the glass slippers, but she could not stop and dashed out of the palace gates at the last stroke of midnight. And there she was in the cold night air, once more the kitchen girl in dirty clothes, with only a single glass slipper to remind her of her happiness.

The Prince was astonished to see her go, and sent a man at once to find her. But the guards at the gate had seen only a poor servant girl running home, and the courtiers found nothing but a glass slipper left behind.

Then the Prince began to search the whole kingdom for the beautiful lady who had made him so happy. From every market-place, the heralds shouted that the King's son would marry the woman whose foot fitted the glass slipper. Princesses tried on the slipper, and then the grand ladies of the court, and then the daughters of rich gentlemen. At last, the royal messenger arrived at Cinderella's home and offered the slipper to the ugly sisters. But no matter how they pushed and shoved, no matter how red they got in the face, they could not force their great boney feet into the little slipper.

Then Cinderella, who had been sent to the back kitchen, came forward and asked: 'Please, may I try it?'

'No, certainly not,' cried the sisters. 'This precious shoe is not for grubby servant girls.'

But the royal messenger looked at her carefully. He noted how graceful and pretty she was, in spite of her clothes. He gave her the

The royal messenger gave her the slipper.

slipper and Cinderella's tiny foot fitted into it as snug as a bird in its nest.

There was a cry of dismay from the ugly sisters, but Cinderella took from under her apron the other glass slipper and put it on. Then everyone was certain that she was the lady of the Prince's heart.

Then, as the step-sisters sobbed and begged to be forgiven for their unkindness, the Fairy Godmother re-appeared. At the touch of her wand Cinderella was changed once more, becoming as beautiful as the moon in a sky full of stars.

Soon after, Cinderella and the Prince were married and lived very happily. She forgave her step-sisters, and to show that her good fortune had not altered her kind heart, she arranged for them to marry two lords of the court, which was perhaps a hard fate for two men who had done no wrong!

Jack decided to try his luck at the top of the beanstalk again.

Jack and
the Beanstalk

THERE was once a poor widow who had a son called Jack and a cow called Milky-white. And all they had to live on was the milk from the cow. But one day Milky-white gave no milk, so the widow told Jack to sell the cow in the market.

Off Jack went and on the road he met a funny-looking man. As they walked along, they began to talk of this and that, and then the man said:

'Well, Jack, you look the sort of chap to make a good bargain. I wonder if you know how many beans make five?'

'Two in each hand and one in the mouth,' says Jack, as sharp as a needle.

'Right you are,' says the man, and pulled five strange-looking beans from his pocket. 'I don't mind making a swop with a smart lad. I'll give these five beans for your cow. Just pop these magic beans in the ground and they'll be up to the sky by next morning.'

So Jack gave him the cow and took the beans back to his mother. But when the widow heard that he had sold the best milker in the parish, not for five pounds, but for five beans, she gave Jack a box on the ears, threw the beans out of the window, and sent her son to bed without supper.

Next morning, Jack thought his room had grown rather dark. And looking out of the window he found the view blocked by huge leaves. So the old fellow on the road had told the truth. The beans were magic. They had sprouted and shot up to the sky in one night.

'Fee-fi-fo-fum, I smell the blood of an Englishman.'

Now Jack was a curious young man, so he took hold of the beanstalk and climbed and climbed and climbed until he reached the sky. And there he found a broad path that led to a great big tall castle, and waiting on the doorstep there was a great big tall woman.

'Morning, mum,' says Jack politely. 'Could you give me some breakfast? I'm as hungry as a hunter.'

'It's breakfast you want, is it?' says the big woman. 'You'll *be* breakfast if you don't move off! My man is an ogre and he loves nothing better than boys fried on toast.'

But the ogre's wife was not a bad sort really, so she took Jack in the kitchen and gave him bread and cheese and a jug of milk. As he was eating, there was a thump! thump! thump! outside that shook the whole house.

'Quick,' cried the ogre's wife, 'it's my old man. Here, jump in the oven and hide.'

Well, that ogre was a big one, to be sure. He threw down three calves for his breakfast. But then he had a sniff around the kitchen, and shouted:

'Fee-fi-fo-fum,
I smell the blood of an Englishman,
Be he alive, or be he dead,
I'll have his bones to grind my bread.'

'Nonsense, dear,' says the wife. 'You're dreaming. Or perhaps you can still smell the little boy I cooked for you yesterday. You run along and wash, and I'll get your breakfast.'

The ogre had his breakfast and rubbed his tummy. Then he took down a couple of bags of gold and began to count the money. As he counted, his head began to nod, and soon he was snoring like a steam-engine. Then Jack crept from the oven, and being a smart young fellow he grabbed a bag of gold from the table and ran helter-skelter to the beanstalk. He threw down the gold and followed as fast as he could, right into his mother's garden.

'Well, mother,' he cried showing her the gold, 'wasn't I right about the beans? They are real magic, you see.'

They lived on that gold for some time. But at last it was finished, and Jack decided to try his luck at the top of the beanstalk once

Jack grabbed the hen and started to run.

more. So up he climbed, and there was the same great big tall woman standing on the doorstep.

'Morning, mum,' says Jack, bold as brass. 'How about something for breakfast?'

Well, the tall woman recognized him, but she wanted to know what had happened to the missing bag of gold, so she took him in and fed him. And again there was a mighty thumping outside, so Jack jumped into the oven. The ogre stamped into the kitchen, wrinkled his nose, and roared:

'Fee-fi-fo-fum,
I smell the blood of an Englishman,
Be he alive, or be he dead,
I'll have his bones to grind my bread.'

But his wife cooked him three oxen for breakfast and soothed him. After breakfast, he rubbed his tummy and began to play with a pet hen. 'Lay, little hen,' said the ogre, and the hen laid an egg that was all of gold. The egg rolled on the table, and the ogre's head began to nod, and soon he was snoring again, as loud as a buzz-saw.

Then Jack crept out of the oven, grabbed the hen, and started to run. But the hen gave a cackle that woke the ogre.

'Wife, wife,' he cried, 'where's my golden hen?'

But by that time Jack had reached the top of the beanstalk, and he tumbled down home like a house on fire.

For a while, Jack was happy, but then he began to wonder what other good things he could find in the ogre's castle. So up the beanstalk he climbed again. This time, he knew better than to go straight to the door. He hid behind a bush, and when he saw that the coast was clear, he nipped into the kitchen and got into the great big copper.

At breakfast time, the ogre came thumping home, and again he thought he could smell a nice tasty boy.

'Fee-fi-fo-fum,' he cried out to his wife, 'I smell the blood of an Englishman. I tell you, wife, I smell him, I smell him.'

And his wife answered: 'It's that young rogue, the one who took your gold and stole your golden hen. I bet he's hiding in the oven.'

But luckily Jack was not there. Then they searched the room,

Jack took a mighty swing at the beanstalk.

but forgot to look in the copper, so they didn't find him. At last, the ogre settled down to his breakfast of three sheep, and then he called for his golden harp.

'Sing!' he ordered the harp, and it began to sing most beautifully. And as it sang, the ogre's head began to nod and he fell asleep. The harp stopped, and all you could hear instead were snores like thunder.

Very quietly, Jack lifted the copper-lid and crept like a mouse to the table. He snatched up the golden harp and ran for the door. But the harp called out 'Master, Master!' and the ogre awoke to see Jack sprinting down the path. With a roar, the ogre was after him, but Jack was speedy and had a good start, and he got to the beanstalk twenty yards in front. Jack leapt onto the beanstalk, but the ogre didn't like the look of it. He thought he would test his weight first. But the harp started crying 'Master, Master!' again. So the ogre took hold of the beanstalk, which shook under him, and down went Jack and down went the ogre.

Now Jack was very nippy, and he just flew down the beanstalk. And as he came close to the ground, he began shouting:

'Mother, mother, bring me an axe, bring me an axe.'

His mother ran out with the axe, but she stopped with fright when she saw the great legs of the ogre coming through the clouds. But Jack jumped to her side, seized the axe, and took a mighty swing at the beanstalk. The beanstalk quivered and swayed, and the ogre, who did not feel too safe, stopped to see what was wrong. Then Jack took another chop, cutting the beanstalk right in half, so that it began to fall. The ogre fell too, like a boulder down a mountain, and his landing made the earth tremble. And there he lay in the widow's garden, with his feet in the air, quite dead.

Then Jack stayed at home with the golden harp and the golden eggs, and he and his mother became very rich. In time, Jack married a beautiful lady, and they lived happily ever after.

The Princess and the Pea

THERE was once a Prince who wished to marry, but the bride he
was looking for had to be really and truly a Princess.

So he travelled right round the world to find one, but wherever
he looked there was always something wrong. There were plenty of
Princesses, to be sure. But were they *real* Princesses? Every lady
he met seemed to be not quite right. At last, he had to come home,
and he was very sad, because he wanted a real Princess so badly.

One evening, there was a terrible storm. There was thunder and
lightning, and the rain came down in torrents. It was a fearful
night, as dark as pitch and dangerous. In the middle of the storm,
somebody knocked at the gate, and the old King himself went to
open it.

A lady stood outside in an awful mess. She was pale and
shivering. Her hair was plastered to her head, and her clothes were
all bedraggled, soaked through with the rain. She looked in a sorry
state, but she said she was a Princess, in fact a *real* Princess.

'We'll soon see about that,' thought the old Queen, but she said
nothing. She went into the bedroom, took off the bedclothes and
laid a pea on the bedstead. Then she took twenty mattresses and
piled them on top of the pea, and then twenty feather-beds on top of
the mattresses.

That was the bed the Princess slept in. And next morning they
all asked her if she had slept well.

'Oh, I had a horrid night,' said the Princess. 'I hardly closed my

She slept on twenty mattresses but still felt the pea.

eyes the whole night! Heaven knows what was in the bed. I seemed to be lying on some hard thing, and my whole body is black and blue this morning. I can't tell you how I've suffered!'

Then they saw at once that she must be a real Princess. She had slept on twenty mattresses and twenty feather-beds but she had still felt the pea. Nobody but a real Princess could have such a delicate skin.

So the Prince married her, for he was sure that he had found a real Princess. And the pea was put into the Museum, where it may still be seen, if no one has stolen it.

Now didn't that lady have the most delicate feelings?

The clever young man didn't want to share his food.

The Golden Goose

THERE was a man who had three sons, and the youngest son was not very bright. People called him Dunderhead, because they thought he was more than half a fool, and they made fun of him and were usually unkind.

One day, when the eldest son was going to the forest to cut wood, his mother gave him a nice little pie and a bottle of wine. As he went into the woods, he met a little old man who greeted him and said:

'Give me a piece of your pie and a little wine, for I'm hungry and thirsty.'

But this clever young man answered:

'Give you some of my food? No thank you. What would I eat myself?'

And away he went. But when he began to chop down a tree, his axe slipped and cut his leg, and then he had to limp home.

Next day, the second son went to the woods with another nice little pie and a bottle of wine. And on the way he met the same old man, who again asked for something to eat and drink. But this son said:

'The more for you, the less for me. So be off with you.'

But when he, too, began to chop wood, the axe jumped off the log and bit into his leg, so that he also limped home with his wound.

Now the next day, since both of his brothers were hurt, Dunderhead was allowed to go to the woods. But his mother gave him only

a crust of dried bread and a bottle of sour beer. The little old man
was waiting for him, and when he asked for food and drink,
Dunderhead said at once:

'I've only got dry bread and stale beer, but if that suits you, let's
sit down and share it together.

As they sat down to eat, Dunderhead found that his bread had
turned to good meat and his beer to fine wine. They ate and drank
with great delight, and then the little man said:

'Since you have a kind heart, and have shared everything with
me, I'll send you a blessing. When you cut down that old tree, you'll
find something valuable at the root.

Then the old man said goodbye and left.

Dunderhead set to work, and when the tree was down he found,
under the roots, a goose with feathers of gold. He felt tired after his
work, so instead of going home he went for the night to an inn by
the roadside.

Dunderhead found a goose with feathers of gold.

Now the landlord had three daughters, and when they saw the wonderful goose each daughter wanted to steal one of the golden feathers. The eldest waited until the young man was in bed, then she grabbed the goose by the wing. But there, to her amazement, she stuck fast, unable to move hand or finger. The second daughter then crept up, but as soon as she reached out a hand to her sister, she too was stuck. Up came the youngest girl, but her sisters cried out, 'Keep away! Keep away!'

'Ha,' thought the third daughter, 'so my sisters want all the feathers for themselves.'

And putting out her hand to her sisters, she found she was just as stuck as they were. And that is how they stayed until the morning.

Next morning, Dunderhead got up, put the goose under his arm, and off he went cheerfully, with the three girls forced to follow him. In the middle of a field, they all met the parson who, seeing three girls running after a young man, cried:

'Shame on you, you young hussies, chasing a young fellow like that!'

The parson cried: 'Shame on you, chasing a fellow like that!'

And reaching out to pull the youngest girl away, he too hung fast, and was dragged along at the end of the line at a pace that made his old feet hurt.

Soon the parson's clerk came by, and he was astonished to see his master hurrying along with a line of girls.

'Hold on, your reverence,' he cried. 'Have you forgotten that you've got a christening to do today?'

He caught hold of the parson's gown, and then he too was stuck.

At that moment two labourers were coming from work, so the parson called out to them for help. They took hold of the clerk, meaning to pull him free, and then they also were stuck.

So there they were, all seven of them in a line, all running after young Dunderhead and his goose.

Now Dunderhead thought he would see a little of the world before he went home, so he took his goose, and his line of followers, to the city. In this city, there lived a King who had one daughter, and this Princess was so sad and serious nobody had ever made her laugh. The King was worried by her miserable looks, and he made it known that the person who should make her laugh would have her for his wife.

It just happened that the Princess was looking out of her window when Dunderhead came to town. And when she saw a merry young man with a golden goose under his arm, and behind him a sorry line of seven people, all stumbling and tripping and treading on each other's heels, she suddenly burst out laughing.

Then Dunderhead took the Princess for his wife, and lived long and happily. But what became of the goose, its golden feathers, and its unlucky followers, no one could ever tell.

The Sleeping Beauty

THERE was once a fortunate country where the King and the Queen had everything they wanted, except a child. After many weary years, of vows and pilgrimages and taking holy water, after visits to wise men and doctors and magicians, the Queen at last gave birth to a daughter.

In their joy, the royal parents arranged a most magnificent christening. And they naturally invited all the local fairies to come and give blessings and gifts to the baby. But unhappily, in the rush and excitement one fairy was forgotten. This was a bad-tempered old lady who lived in a far part of the kingdom who, hearing of the feast, decided to come anyway, invited or not.

At the christening, the fairies stepped up to make their gifts. One by one, they promised to make the baby beautiful, and gentle, and clever, and kind. But the uninvited old lady was in a spiteful mood, and when her turn came she promised that the baby girl would one day prick her finger with a spindle, and die.

There was silence. Then there were groans and weeping. The Queen fainted. But a younger, kind-hearted fairy, having pity on the innocent baby, came forward and said:

'I cannot undo the curse, but I can make it less terrible. The child will prick her finger, but she will not die. Instead, she will sleep for a hundred years, until a King's son awakes her.'

Well, you can imagine what care they took to protect the Princess! She was watched and guarded, and spindles were forbidden everywhere, on pain of death. So the Princess grew up as beautiful and as good as the fairies had promised. But she was a bright, lively girl also; and when one day, at the age of fifteen, she came upon a strange old woman spinning in a far, forgotten attic of the palace, the Princess wanted to try her hand at this unusual task. As she reached for the spindle, it pricked her finger and she fell down unconscious at once.

People ran from all over the palace. They rubbed her and bathed her and tried to give her medicine. But it was no good. She was in a deep swoon. So they took her and sadly laid her in a golden bed, and if you held your ear to her mouth you could still just hear her soft breathing. In her gown of lace, she looked like an angel asleep. Then the good fairy came and touched with her wand all the people and things of the palace (except the King and Queen), so that everything would rest as it was until the Princess awoke. The roasting partridges in the kitchen were stilled on the spit. The great horses were like statues in the stables. The guards stood by the doors and snored quietly, while the little pet dog was curled at the foot of the Princess's bed.

The King and the Queen kissed their dear child and left the palace. As they went, a forest of wild trees and thorns and giant brambles shot up, hiding everything except the tops of the highest towers. The palace was abandoned. It became a place of mystery, and at last was almost forgotten.

Now a hundred years went by and the King and Queen were long dead. And then a Prince from another land came to hunt nearby. He saw the towers peeping from the dark forest, but no one knew what this place was. At last, a very old farmer remembered the tales his grandfather had told him, and he was able to tell the Prince about the Sleeping Beauty and about the man who would wake her in time. At once, the Prince decided that he was the person to wake her, and he thrust his way through the forest already half in love with the waiting Princess.

His men were afraid, but the Prince was young and brave. As he pushed into the forest, the thorns and creepers unwound themselves, and a path opened towards the palace. In the courtyard he found a strange, unnatural silence. Men and animals were frozen as if in death. But the coats of the animals shone with good health,

The Prince decided that he was the person to wake her.

and the faces of many of the men were fat and red, as if they had just finished feasting. The Prince climbed marble steps into rooms free from dust and cobwebs. Soldiers were leaning on their muskets, and one mumbled in his sleep. The Prince went into a room of gold, and there on the golden bed lay a maiden with lips like coral and skin as pure and white as fresh snow.

In wonder, the Prince knelt by the bed. With his lips he touched the forehead of the beautiful young face.

'Is that you, dear Prince?' the girl murmured, coming awake with a little start. 'I have been expecting you for so long!'

Then the two young people laughed and cried and swore that they loved each other. Suddenly, the palace came alive. Men yawned and stretched. Servants, stopped in mid-stride, bustled about their business. The cooks went on with the meal. The Princess's parrot screamed, and the pet dog by her feet stirred and scratched.

In wonder, the Prince knelt by the bed.

Then the Prince raised the Sleeping Beauty from the bed, and led her out, into the lively palace. The feast was served and the violins played, and they took such joy in each other that they decided to be married. And so they were, that very same night.

Next morning, the Prince left, to return to his own land. He told his parents that he had been lost and spent the night in a poor cottage. His father believed him but his mother, the Queen, was not sure. And she became more suspicious as her son spent more and more time away from home. For two years the Prince secretly visited his Princess whenever he could, and they had two children. The elder was a daughter called Morning and the younger a handsome boy called Day.

Now the Queen was really an Ogre, and loved to eat young children, though her son did not know this. While her husband lived, she kept her nasty vice hidden. But when the old King died, and the young Prince became the new ruler and brought his secret Princess and his two children to the palace to live with him, the wicked Queen-Mother, in her jealousy, planned to kill and eat her son's young family.

While the new King was busy far away, his mother sent her daughter-in-law and the children to a house in the country. And there she ordered the cook to kill the little girl, Morning, and to serve her for dinner with a French sauce. The cook was terrified of the Ogre-Queen, so he took his big knife to the nursery. But little Morning was so sweet and gentle that the good man wept and dropped his knife. He took the child to his wife, with orders to hide her, and then he prepared a lamb and served it to the Queen-Mother with a strong sauce.

A while later, the wicked Queen fancied another dish of meat and ordered the cook to kill the little boy Day. Day was fencing with a monkey, and again the cook could not bear to kill him. Again, he took the child in his arms to his wife, and served the kid of a goat to the hungry Queen. The meat was very tender and the cruel Ogre found it wonderfully good.

And then the Queen-Mother thought: 'I'll eat my daughter-in-law too!'

This time the cook was shaking with fear and felt he must obey. He took his knife and he went to the young Queen and explained what he must do. The sad Queen, who thought that her pretty babes were dead, only held out her neck and said:

'Do it, do it, so that I may join my poor little babies.'

At this, the cook wept again, and could not kill her. He told her that the children were safe and he took the Queen to meet them, hidden away in his wife's house. Then he prepared for the Queen-Mother a dish of venison, which she ate with much smacking of the lips.

Now the wicked old Queen was happy! When her son, the young King, returned from far away, she told him that mad wolves had attacked his wife and children in the forest and eaten them up. And she thought in her wicked heart: Good riddance to them all!

But one day, walking in the country, the Queen-Mother heard voices playing near a cottage hidden in the woods. With a shock, she thought she recognized the voices. And sure enough, entering the simple house, she found the children and her beautiful daughter-in-law, all of whom she had hoped were dead. In a rage, she ordered all three to be bound and dragged to the palace, where a great cauldron of snakes was prepared into which she would hurl her innocent victims. But just as the cauldron was ready, the King came riding home unexpectedly. With a tremendous shout of joy he saw his beloved missing family, and he rushed towards them.

Then the wicked old Queen saw that all was lost. With a cry of rage and spite, she dived into the cauldron. She disappeared under the writhing snakes and was bitten to death.

The King clutched his wife and his children to his heart and he promised never to leave them again. Nor did he. And they lived happily ever after.

The giant thought nothing of carrying six oxen on his back.

Jack the Giant-killer

IN the time of King Arthur, there lived near the Land's End, in the county of Cornwall, a farmer with a son called Jack. Jack was a bright, lively lad, and nothing could get the better of him.

In those days, the Mount of Cornwall was kept by a huge giant, about eighteen feet high and three yards around, whose grim face was a terror to everyone. He lived in a cave in the middle of the Mount, and he used to wade over to the mainland and take what he wished. He seized the cattle, and thought nothing of carrying six oxen on his back, while hogs and sheep hung from his belt like bunches of candles. He had plundered the land for many years, and all Cornwall was in despair.

One day, when the council in the townhall were talking yet again about the giant, Jack entered and said:

'What reward will you give to the man who kills the Giant Cormoran?'

'All the giant's treasure,' they answered.

'That's for me,' said Jack, 'so I'll do it.'

He got a horn, shovel and pickaxe, and went to the Mount on a dark winter's evening. He dug a pit as broad and as long as the giant, and covered it over to look like the ground. Then he raised his horn and blew a blast that had the giant rushing from his cave.

'Who dares disturb my sleep?' roared the giant. 'I'll have you whole and grilled for breakfast.'

But the giant did not look where he was going, and tumbled into

73

the pit with a shock that shook the mountain. Then Jack took the pickaxe and gave him a mighty knock right on the crown of the head, and struck him dead. Jack took the treasure and returned in triumph to the town. The people were so glad, they called him 'Jack the Giant-Killer' and have him a sword and a belt on which were written, in letters of gold:

Here's the right valiant Cornish man,
Who slew the Giant Cormoran.

The news of Jack's victory soon spread, and the nation of the giants vowed to be revenged. Soon after, when Jack was on his travels, he lay down in a wood near the castle of the Giant Blunderbore. While Jack was sleeping, the giant came by, and reading on the belt that this was the famous Giant-Killer, picked Jack up and carried him away. When they entered the castle, Jack awoke, and saw all around human bones. Blunderbore tossed Jack into a dungeon, and as the giant left, Jack heard a voice cry:

'Do what you can to get away,
Or you'll become the giant's prey.
He's gone to fetch his brother, who
Will kill and likewise torture you.'

In the corner of the dark room, Jack found some strong ropes that lay there forgotten. He made nooses at the end of two ropes. Then waiting at the window for the return of the giant brothers, he threw the ropes over their heads as they unlocked the gates, and pulled with all his might. They went black in the face. Then Jack slid down the ropes, and with his sword he slew them both. With the keys of the castle, which he took from Blunderbore's pocket, he unlocked another dungeon, and found there three ladies, almost starved to death. Blunderbore had killed their husbands, and left the ladies tied by their hair to the roof.

'Sweet ladies,' said Jack, 'I have destroyed the monster and his brother, and now you are free.'

He gave them the keys to the castle, and went on his way to Wales.

He travelled fast, but soon lost the path. He was wandering around, looking for the right road, when he came to a large house

in a narrow valley. He knocked on the door. To his surprise, it was answered by a giant with two heads. But unlike the Cornish giants, this Welsh one was a tricky, cunning brute, who invited Jack in with a show of smiles, and took him to a bedroom. But Jack did not sleep, and in the night he heard a muttering through the wall:

> 'Though here you lodge with me this night,
> You shall not see the morning light.
> My club shall dash your brains outright.'

'Is that so?' thought Jack. 'If that's one of your Welsh tricks, I'll be ready for you.'

He took a lump of wood and laid it in the bed instead of him. Then, in the darkest hour, the giant crept in and beat the bed with his largest club. But hidden in the corner of the room, Jack was laughing in his sleeve.

Next morning, Jack came down to breakfast with many thanks for his night's rest.

'How did you sleep?' said the giant. 'Did you feel nothing in the night?'

'Oh,' said Jack, 'nothing but a rat, that gave me a couple of slaps with its tail.'

The giant was amazed, but he put the breakfast on the table and poured into Jack's plate four gallons of porridge. Now Jack was too clever to let the giant see that he could not eat it, so he cunningly spooned the porridge into a leather bag he had below his coat. Then, offering to show the giant a trick, he took a knife and plunged it into the bag of porridge, pretending it was his belly.

'Odds-bods,' cried the giant, 'why, that's nothing. I can do that very same trick myself.'

So taking a knife, he ripped up his belly from top to bottom, and fell down dead.

Now, at this same time, King Arthur's son was travelling in Wales, looking for a beautiful lady possessed by seven evil spirits. He had with him a large chest of money, to pay for his journey. But when he stopped at a certain market town, he found that the people had arrested a corpse, because of sums of money that the dead man had owed in his life. The Prince was shocked by this cruelty, and paid off the debts, although this left him with but twopence for himself.

Jack was taken with the generosity of the Prince, and offered to be his servant. And since the Prince soon gave his last twopence to a poor old woman, they set out with nothing. Lacking a place for the night, Jack suggested they go to his uncle nearby. But this uncle was a giant with three heads, able to defeat five hundred men in armour.

'Alas,' said the Prince, 'he'll certainly chop us up in a mouthful. We're hardly enough to fill one of his hollow teeth.'

But Jack was not afraid, and galloped off to knock at the giant's gate.

'Who's there?' the giant roared like thunder.

'Your poor nephew Jack, dear uncle,' Jack replied. 'I've come with heavy news. The King's son is a-coming, with a thousand men in armour, to kill you and destroy your lands.'

'That's bad indeed,' said the giant. 'Nephew, you must help me. I will run and hide. You must lock me in and keep the keys until this Prince has gone.'

So Jack locked the giant in a hiding-place, and that night he and the Prince made merry in the castle. And next morning, when the Prince was on the road with treasure from the castle vaults, Jack

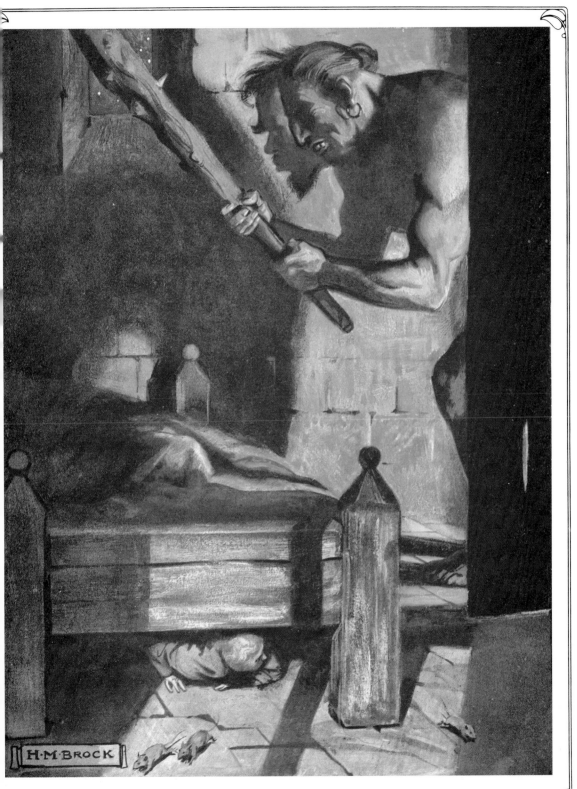

The giant beat the bed with his largest club.

let out the giant. The monster was so pleased to be saved from the Prince and his terrible army that he offered his nephew a reward.

'Well,' said Jack, 'I want nothing but the coat and cap, the old rusty sword and the slippers that are by your bed.'

'These are my most precious things,' said the giant. 'The coat makes you invisible, the cap is the cap of knowledge, the sword will cut even the hardest things, and the slippers will speed you like the wind. But you have saved me from death and destruction, and you may take them with all my heart.'

Jack hurried after the Prince and together they arrived at the house of the beautiful lady with the evil spirits. When she knew the Prince had come to save her, the evil in her heart set him a test. She wiped her mouth with a handkerchief then hid it in her bosom, saying:

'Show me the handkerchief in the morning, or else you will die.'

The Prince was sad, but Jack put on the cap of knowledge and knew what to do. In the night, when the lady flew to visit her demon spirit Jack was there before her, carried by his shoes of swiftness and invisible in his magic coat. He stole the hand-kerchief from the demon, and took it to the Prince, who gave it to the lady in the morning.

The lady was angry, and at once made another test. She kissed the Prince on the lips and ordered him to bring her next morning the lips she had kissed in the night. Then away she flew again to her demon, and kissed him.

'This is too hard for the King's son,' she told the demon. 'I have kissed you, and how shall he bring me your lips?'

But Jack was standing there unseen, and with a single stroke he cut off the demon's head, put it under his invisible coat, and brought it to his master. In the morning, the Prince took the head by its horns and held it before the lady.

Then the evil magic was broken, and the bad spirits left the lady. She appeared now in all gentleness and beauty, and married the Prince on that same day. They all returned to the court of King Arthur, where Jack, for his many great and famous adventures, was made one of the Knights of the Round Table.

The twelve Princesses danced until the morning.

The Twelve
Dancing Princesses

THERE was once a King who had twelve beautiful daughters. They all slept in the same room, and when they went to bed the doors were locked. But every morning their shoes were quite worn out, as if they had been dancing all night. But nobody knew how this happened.

The King was worried, so he offered a reward to anyone who could find out the secret. The person who could tell where the Princesses were dancing could marry the Princess he liked best, and be the next King of the country. But whoever tried and failed would, after three days and nights, be put to death.

The first man to try was a King's son. He decided to watch all night. But he took a glass of wine and soon fell asleep, and when he awoke in the morning he found the Princesses in their beds with their shoes once more as thin as paper. This happened on the other two nights also, so the King had his head cut off.

After this, many other great gentlemen tried. But they all had no luck and they all lost their lives.

Now, an old soldier, wounded in the wars, was passing through that land. On a path through the woods he met an old woman who stopped for a chat, and she asked him how he was doing.

'Not much is going right for me,' answered the soldier, 'but I'd like to find out about those Princesses and their dancing, then I might become King.'

'Well,' said the old dame, 'that's easy enough. You've been

TAY·NIELSEN·1912

friendly to me so I'll help you. Take this magic cloak, and remember not to drink the wine they will give you at night. Pretend to be asleep, but when the Princesses get up, slip on this cloak which will make you invisible. Then you can follow them.'

At the palace, the King welcomed the soldier, and entertained him. Then, at nightfall, the soldier settled down on a couch just outside the Princesses' door. One of the sisters brought him a glass of wine, but the cunning old soldier had fixed a sponge under the collar of his coat, and when he seemed to drink he was really pouring the wine into that sponge. Then he lay down and began to snore very loudly.

'Another foolish fellow,' said the eldest Princess laughing. 'He's come to lose his head!'

Then all the sisters got up quietly and dressed in their finest clothes, skipping about, as if they could hardly wait to begin dancing. But the youngest was uneasy.

'I don't know what it is,' she said, 'but I feel something is about to go wrong.'

'Silly girl,' said the eldest, 'do you think this simple soldier can succeed where Princes have failed? Why, the fellow is already snoring from the drugged wine I gave him.'

Then the eldest Princess clapped her hands and a trapdoor beneath her bed flew open. One by one, the sisters went down, and the soldier, who had been pretending to sleep and had heard everything, put on his cloak and followed. But on the stairs he got too close to the youngest and trod on her long dress.

'Someone has hold of my gown,' she cried. But the eldest replied: 'Hush, you fool. It's only a nail on the wall.'

At the bottom of the steps, they came to a strange grove of underground trees, where the leaves were of silver and glittered like summer rain. The soldier, wanting some proof of this wonderful journey, snapped off a little branch, which cracked loudly.

'What was that noise?' said the youngest. 'I'm sure something is wrong.' But the eldest answered: 'Hush, it's only our Princes, calling for us to come.'

Then they came to another grove of golden leaves, and another of diamonds. And at each, the soldier broke off a branch, with a noise that made the youngest Princess tremble. But her eldest sister soothed her, and they went on to the shore of a great lake, where twelve handsome Princes were waiting in twelve little boats.

As a Princess stepped into each boat, the soldier got in with the youngest.

'Is it the weather?' said the youngest Prince, 'but this boat seems
very hard to row tonight.'

'Yes,' said the Princess, 'I certainly feel rather warm.'

They rowed across the lake to a palace where the lights were twinkling and the music was playing. They stepped into the ball-room and each Prince began to dance with his Princess. And the old soldier, who was a cheerful soul and still invisible, had a dance too. It made him thirsty, so whenever a glass of wine was set down, he picked it up and drained it. When the youngest sister saw the wine disappearing in this ghostly manner, she was frightened once more. But the eldest told her not to be silly, and to get on with the dance.

They danced until three o'clock in the morning, but by then their shoes had holes in them, so they all had to leave. The Princes rowed them back across the lake and left them on the far shore, promising to return again the next night.

Then the old soldier ran ahead of the ladies, climbed the stairs, took off his cloak, and jumped into bed. He was snoring as the twelve sisters came slowly and wearily into their bedroom. They smiled at each other, thinking they were still safe. Tired and happy, they went to sleep, and at the foot of each bed stood a pair of worn-out shoes.

Next morning, the old soldier said nothing. But he was so pleased with the dancing, and the wine, that he went back with the sisters for two more nights, and had a very good time. And when he left the underground palace on the last night, he took a gold cup with him, as another proof of his journey.

On the morning of the fourth day, the soldier was taken before the King.

'Have you found out,' said the King, 'where my twelve daughters dance at night? Think carefully, or else you will die.'

'I have,' said the soldier. 'They dance with twelve Princes in a wonderful palace below the ground. And to show that I speak the truth, I have brought these things from my journey there.'

Then he showed the King the little branches of silver and gold and diamonds, and he gave him the golden cup. The King called for his daughters, and when they saw what the soldier had done they knew it was no good denying what had happened. So they told their father everything.

The old soldier had his reward, and since he was no youngster himself, he chose to marry the eldest Princess, who suited him very well.

Rumpel-Stilts-Ken and the miller's daughter.

Rumpel-Stilts-Ken

DOWN by the river, in a certain country, there was once a miller. The miller was poor but his daughter was very beautiful and she was also very clever and shrewd besides. The miller was so proud of her that one day, when the royal court came hunting nearby, he told the King that his daughter could spin straw into gold.

Now the King was fond of money, so he ordered the girl to be brought to the palace at once. He led her to a room where there was a great heap of straw, gave her a spinning-wheel, and said:

'If you love your life, spin all this into gold by tomorrow morning.'

The poor girl cried that she could not do it, but it was no use. The door was locked, and she was left alone.

She sat in a corner and began to weep, when suddenly the door opened and a funny-looking man came hobbling in.

'Good day, miss,' he said, 'and why are you weeping?'

'Alas,' she answered, 'I must spin this straw into gold, and I don't know how.'

'What will you give me,' said the little fellow, 'to do it for you?'

'My necklace,' said the maiden.

So he agreed, and sat himself down at the wheel, and whistled and sang. Round and about the wheel went merrily, and quickly the work was done and the gold all spun.

Next morning, when the King saw this, he was astonished and

The miller was very proud of his beautiful daughter.

pleased. But it made him even more greedy, and he took the girl to a larger room, with a larger pile of straw, and told her to spin it into gold, or to lose her life. And as she began to weep, the little fellow opened the door again, and asked her what she would give to have the task done?

'The ring on my finger,' said she.

So he took the ring and whistled and sang. Round and about the wheel went merrily, till by morning the work was all done.

The King was delighted with all this shining treasure, but still it was not enough for him. He took the girl to a still larger room, and said:

'All this must be spun tonight, and if it is you shall be my Queen.' But that evening, when the little dwarf came and offered to help her, she said she had nothing left to give him.

'In that case,' he said, 'promise me your first child when you are Queen.'

'That may never be,' thought the miller's daughter. But as she knew no other way to spin the gold, she did promise. And then the little man sang, and the wheel spun merrily, and the task was done. And when the King came in the morning, he was forced to keep his word. He married the miller's daughter, and she really did become Queen.

She soon forgot her promise, and when her first child was born she was glad. But one day, as she was playing with her baby, the dwarf stepped into the room to remind her. Then her heart was sore and she offered him all the treasure of the kingdom to let her keep the baby. She wept and wept, until at last her tears softened him a little, and he said:

'I'll give you three days. If in that time you can tell me my name, you can keep the child.'

Now the Queen lay awake at night, thinking of every name she had ever heard. And she sent messengers all over the land, to find out new ones. Next day, when the little fellow came, she began with Timothy, Benjamin, Jeremy, and all the other names she had thought of. But each time he answered: 'That's not my name.'

The second day, she tried strange and comical names, like, Bandylegs, Hunchback, Crookshanks, but still he said: 'That's not my name.'

She sent messengers all over the land to find out new names.

On the third day, when her messengers returned, one of them said:

'I don't know any more names. But yesterday, as I was climbing a hill in the forest, where the fox and hare say good night to each other, I saw a funny little man hopping on one leg in front of a fire, and he was singing:

> Merry is the feast I'll make,
> Today I'll brew, tomorrow bake.
> Merrily I'll dance and sing,
> For next day will a stranger bring.
> Little does my lady dream
> Rumpel-Stilts-Ken is my name.'

When the Queen heard this, she jumped for joy and received the little man with her baby in her arms and all her court around her.

'Now then,' said the funny-looking dwarf, 'what's my name?'

'Is it John?'

'No, it's not.'

'Is it Tom?'

'No, not that.'

'Is it Jemmy?'

'Not that either,' said the dwarf, with a wicked grin, because he thought he had won the child.

'Well now,' said the Queen, 'can your name be Rumpel-Stilts-Ken?'

'Some witch must have told you,' shouted the little fellow in anger. In his rage, he stamped his foot right through the floor, deep into the ground. And so fiercely did he pull to get himself free, that he split himself quite in two, and that was the end of him.

In his rage he stamped his foot right through the floor.

Hansel and Gretel

THERE was once a poor woodcutter who lived in the forest with his wife and his two children by a former marriage. The children were called Hansel and Gretel. But times were hard for the woodcutter, and there was less and less to eat in his house.

'What will become of us, wife?' the poor man sighed one night. 'How will we find enough to live on and feed the children?'

Then his wife replied that they must take the children away, to the wildest part of the woods, and give them some bread and light a fire and leave them. At first, the man could not find it in his heart to abandon his children to the beasts of the forest. But his wife said:

'You fool, then we must all die. You had better start making our coffins.'

So the woodcutter sadly agreed to do what his wife wanted.

But the boy and girl, unable to sleep from hunger, heard what their stepmother said. The little girl cried, but Hansel said:

'Hush, Gretel, I will help you.'

In the night, when all was quiet, he got up and slipped out of the back door. He looked for white pebbles that shone like silver under the moon, and he filled his pockets with as many as they would hold. Then he crept back into bed and said to Gretel: 'Sleep in peace, dear sister. All will be well.'

Next morning, at sunrise, the wife woke the children, saying they were all going to the forest to chop wood. She gave them each a piece of bread, warning them not to eat it too soon, and they set out.

As they went, Hansel kept stopping till his father asked him why he did so.

'Oh father,' said Hansel, 'I'm saying goodbye to my white cat, sitting on the roof of our house.'

'Fool,' cried the wife, 'that's not a cat, but only the sun shining on the chimney.'

But Hansel, each time he stopped, dropped a pebble on the path.

They reached the middle of the woods and made a great fire. Then the man and his wife left the children, promising to return later. As the children sat by the fire, they heard a branch knocking on a hollow tree. Thinking it was their father's axe, they felt safe, so they ate and waited quietly. Then, as it grew late, the weary children fell asleep, and when they awoke it was dark. Gretel began to cry, but Hansel comforted her.

'Wait till the moon rises,' he said, 'then I'll lead you home.'

And when the moon came up, he took her hand and followed the pebbles, which gleamed like silver coins, leading straight to their house.

The woodcutter welcomed them back with joy, though the wife scolded them for staying out so late. But the bad times continued for the family, until the wife said again:

'There's half a loaf to eat, and then we are finished. We must take the children even deeper into the woods, and leave them.'

The husband who agrees the first time will also give way the second. Sadly, the woodcutter prepared to leave for the forest.

Again, the children could not sleep and heard their stepmother. But this time she had barred the door, and Hansel could collect no pebbles.

Early next morning, off they went to the forest, with even smaller pieces of bread in their pockets. As they walked along, Hansel was secretly crumbling the bread. Then he stopped every few yards, to drop some crumbs by the path, so that his father had to urge him on.

'Oh father,' he said, 'I'm looking at my little dove, nodding to me from the roof.'

'Fool,' cried the wife, 'it's only the sun shining on the chimney.'

But Hansel kept dropping the crumbs.

Deep in the forest they lit another fire, and then the parents left.

After a while, the children slept. But when they awoke in the dark, and Hansel tried to follow the crumbs home, he found that the birds had eaten them. They were lost. For three days they wandered through the woods, eating berries and wild fruits, but growing so tired and so sad.

Then, just as they thought they would die of cold and hunger, they saw a snow-white bird which sang to them so sweetly that they followed it. And very soon they came to a cottage made of bread and cakes, with windows of clear sugar. They were so hungry, Hansel reached for a piece of the roof, and Gretel took a bite at the window. As they were eating, they heard a voice calling:

'Tip-tap, tip-tap, who is rapping at my door?'

And the children answered: 'The wind, the wind, only the child of heaven.' And they went on eating.

Then a very old woman came out of the door on crutches, and welcomed the frightened children to her house. She led them inside and fed them milk and pancakes, apples and nuts, and when they had eaten their fill she showed them two nice little beds, as soft as down. So Hansel and Gretel climbed into bed and thought they were in heaven.

But the old woman, who seemed so kind, was really a wicked witch. She used her house of bread and cakes to tempt little children, and when they came to nibble, she caught them and cooked them and ate them. Witches have red eyes and cannot see well. But like wild animals they have a fine sense of smell and can sniff children from far away.

While Hansel and Gretel were sleeping, the witch poked their pretty red cheeks and mumbled: 'That will make a tasty bite.' Then she took hold of Hansel and shut him in a cage and paid no attention to his cries. As for Gretel, the poor child was set to work, and her main task was to cook for her brother, to fatten him up for the witch's pot.

Each morning, the witch visited the cage.

'Hansel,' she said, 'stretch out your finger. I want to see if you are fat enough yet.'

But Hansel held out a bone, and the witch, who had such bad sight, felt it and could not understand why the child remained so thin. At last, she could wait no longer.

A very old woman welcomed the frightened children to her house.

She took hold of Hansel and shut him in a cage.

'Gretel,' she cried in a rage, 'heat the water. Fat or thin, Hansel shall be cooked today.'

How poor Gretel wept as she put the pot on the flames! 'And now,' said the witch, 'we'll get the pie ready. Creep into the oven, girl, and see if it's hot enough.' For the evil old woman meant to push Gretel into the oven and eat her as well. But Gretel said:

'How do I get in?'

'Though the door, stupid goose,' answered the witch. 'The opening is quite big enough. Look, even I can get in.'

And the witch put her head though the oven door. Then Gretel gave her a sudden push, slammed the oven door shut, and stoked up the fire. The witch howled and howled, but Gretel ran out of the kitchen, and the wicked old woman was burned to ashes.

Quickly, Gretel opened her brother's cage, and they put their arms around each other and kissed and cried. When they were sure the witch was dead, they looked all over the house and found trunks full of pearls and diamonds and other precious stones.

'These are better than pebbles,' said Hansel happily. So they filled their pockets and set off home.

The way home was long and difficult. They came to a large river with no bridge, but Gretel sang to a little white duck so sweetly that the bird gladly swam with them across the water. They went on and at last came to a part of the woods that they recognized. And there, at the end of the path, was their own dear home. They ran joyfully into the house, and found that their stepmother had died and that their father had wept for them every day since he had left them in the forest.

They kissed their father, and Gretel shook from her apron the pearls and diamonds from the witch's trunk. Hansel emptied his pockets and precious stones sparkled in the sun.

Then all their sorrows were at an end, and they lived after that as happy as can be.

The Travelling Musicians

ONCE there was an old donkey who had given many long years of service to his master and could work no more. So the farmer thought there was no point in keeping the animal and wanted to put an end to him. But the donkey was a wise old beast, and guessed what his master was thinking.

'I'll run away,' thought the donkey. 'I've got a notable voice, so I'll go to the big city, to become a musician.'

A mile or so down the road, he saw a dog lying in the ditch and panting.

'Why are you panting, my friend?' said the donkey.

'Alas,' said the dog, 'I'm old and weak, and my master was going to knock me on the head because I can't hunt any more. So I'm running away.'

'Come with me,' said the donkey. 'I'm going to the big city to be a musician, and you can try too.'

So the dog got up, and they jogged on together.

A little farther on, they saw a cat, sitting sadly in the road, and they asked what the matter was.

'Ah me,' sighed the cat, 'I'm growing old and my life is in danger. My mistress was going to drown me, because I no longer catch mice. But I ran away, and now what will I do?'

'Come with us to the big city,' said the donkey. 'You are a fine night singer and will make a fortune as a musician.'

So the cat joined the party.

Soon afterwards they met a cock sitting on a gate and crowing away as if he would burst.

'My goodness,' said the donkey, 'that's a famous noise. What's it all about?'

'Why,' said the cock, 'I was just saying that it was fine weather for washing-day, when the cook came up and threatened to cut off my head and make me into soup for the Sunday guests.'

The cat was a fine night singer.

'Lord forbid!' cried the donkey. 'Come along with us. We'll have four good voices here, and if we sing in tune, we'll get plenty of work in the big city.'

And away they went, all four together.

When night came on, they went into a wood to sleep. The donkey and the dog lay down under a tree, the cat climbed into the branches, while the cock flew to the very top. From this height, he had a good look round, to make sure they were safe. In the distance, he saw a light.

'There must be a house over that way,' he called, 'for I can see something bright.'

'Let's make for it,' said the donkey. 'It will be a bit more comfortable lodging than this wood, and we could all do with a bite to eat.'

So they set off towards the light, and came close to a large house in which a gang of robbers was living.

The donkey, being the tallest of the four, went up to the window and peeped in.

'Well, old fellow,' said Chanticler Cock, 'what do you see?'

'I see a table,' answered the donkey, 'spread with all kinds of good things, and some ruffians, who look like thieves, sitting around making merry.'

'That would be a good place for us,' said the dog, 'if only we can get in.'

So they put their heads together to find a way to get the robbers out, and at last they hit on a plan.

The donkey stood upright, with his forefeet against the window. The dog got on his back. The cat scrambled onto the dog's shoulders. And the cock sat on the cat's head. Then, at a signal, they began their music. The donkey brayed, the dog barked, the cat miaowed, and the cock crowed. Then they all dashed through the window at once, and came tumbling into the room amid broken glass and frightful noise. The robbers thought some fearful devil was attacking them, and ran away as fast as they could.

When the robbers were gone, the four travellers sat down and finished the feast. Then they rubbed their tummies, full of so many good things, and went to bed. The donkey stretched himself on a heap of straw in the yard. The dog lay on the mat behind the door. The cat curled up on the hearth in front of the warm ashes. And the cock perched on a beam at the top of the house. Then tired out with their journey, they soon fell asleep.

Now when the robbers saw that the lights were out and all was quiet, they began to think that they had run away too quickly. So the boldest one crept back, to see what was going on. Seeing that all was still, he entered the kitchen and groped for a match in order to light a candle. And mistaking the glowing eyes of the cat for live coals, he thrust the match into the cat's face, hoping to light it.

The cat was highly indignant, and springing up into the robber's face began to scratch and bite. In panic, the robber fled for the back door, but he tripped over the dog on the mat, who snarled and bit him in the leg. The robber stumbled on into the yard, only to get a terrific kick from the donkey. At this row going on below, the cock woke up and crowed with all his might.

In terror, the bold robber ran back to the gang. And this was the story he told the chief.

In the kitchen, there was a witch before the fire, who spat at him

and scratched his face with her long nails. Then a man, hiding behind the door with a knife, had stabbed him in the leg. He had dashed into the yard, but there a black monster with a club struck him a fierce blow. After that, a devil sitting on the top of the house had begun shouting: 'Throw the rascal up here!'

Well, the robbers were so frightened that they never dared go back to that house. But the four musicians were very pleased with their new home and decided to stay there. They never did get to the big city, and for all one knows may still be living in the house in the wood to this day.

Rapunzel

THERE was once a man and his wife who, for many years, longed for a child, and at last it seemed that their wish would come true.

At the back of their house was a very beautiful garden, but they did not dare enter it because it belonged to a witch. But the wife gazed at the garden from her window, and as she looked down on a bed of lovely bellflowers she began to want them very much. They looked so fresh and so green, and their roots tasted so good in a salad.

'Ah, husband,' she said at last, 'unless I can have some of those bellflowers out of the garden I shall surely die.'

Her husband was very frightened. But he loved his wife, and to please her he climbed over the wall at night and got her the bellflowers. The wife found them just as good as she had hoped, and she liked them so much she sent her husband back for more. But this time, as he climbed over the wall, he came face to face with the witch.

'How dare you,' she cried, 'climb my wall and steal my plants. You will be sorry for this.'

The husband shook when he saw the witch. But he explained that his wife had a longing for the bellflowers, and as she was expecting a child he did not want to upset her. Then the witch was less angry and said:

'If that is the case, take as many plants as you wish, but on one condition: you must give me the child when it's born, and I will care for it like a mother.'

The husband was too afraid not to agree. So he took the plants, and when the child was born the witch came and carried the baby away. It was a baby girl, so the witch called her Rapunzel, which is the name for bellflowers in that country.

Rapunzel grew into the prettiest little girl under the sun. But the witch guarded her jealously. When the child was twelve, the witch took her to a dark wood and shut her in a tower with no stairs and no door, and only one little window, right at the very top. When the witch wanted to visit the girl, she cried:

'Rapunzel, Rapunzel,
Let down your hair.'

This time he came face to face with the witch.

And Rapunzel undid her long, long hair, as yellow and fine as gold, and let it fall from the window to the foot of the tower. Then the witch took hold of the hair like a rope and climbed up.

One day, it happened that the King's son came riding through the forest. He saw the strange tower deep in the woods, and as he passed he heard the most beautiful singing. He wanted to enter the tower but he could find no stairs and no door. He went away, but the singing had touched his heart, so nearly every day he returned to the dark wood to listen. Then once, as he stood behind a tree, he saw the witch coming, and heard her call:

'Rapunzel, Rapunzel,
Let down your hair.'

And then the witch climbed up the hair into the tower.

'Well,' thought the Prince, 'if that's the way to do it, I'll try my luck too.'

So he called out:

'Rapunzel, Rapunzel,
Let down your hair.'

In a moment, the long hair came floating down to the foot of the tower and up went the Prince, hand over hand.

The arrival of the Prince made Rapunzel very frightened, for she knew nothing about men. But he talked to her so gently, and was so friendly and kind, that she soon began to like him. They talked and talked, and the Prince told her of all the wonderful things in the world outside the tower. So when he told her that he loved her, she had lost all her fear and saw that he was young and handsome. She put her hand in his, and said:

'I will gladly go with you, but I do not know how to leave this tower. You will have to help me. Come back every day with a strand of silk, which I will twist into a ladder to take me down.'

Now the witch visited Rapunzel by day, and the Prince by night. And the two young people were very happy together. The witch noticed nothing until one day Rapunzel said:

'How is it, mother, that you are so much heavier to pull up than the King's son?'

At once the witch knew that she had been tricked. In her rage,

The witch took hold of the hair like a rope and climbed up.

she seized Rapunzel's long golden hair and – snip, snap! – cut it all off, close to the head. Then the witch kept the hair and drove Rapunzel out of the tower and into the furthest part of the forest, where she had to live with the beasts, in misery and fear.

On the evening of that same day, the Prince arrived as usual, and called:

'Rapunzel, Rapunzel,
Let down your hair.'

Then the cunning old witch tied the hair that she had cut to the window-frame, and let it down. The Prince climbed up, and at the top he found, not his dear Rapunzel, but the old hag full of spite and anger.

'So you've come to fetch your wife,' cried the witch, 'but the pretty bird is no longer in the nest. The cat has got her, and now it will scratch out your eyes. You will never see your Rapunzel again.'

The Prince leaped to the window, trying to escape from the witch. He jumped and fell a long, long way into a thorn bush and the thorns scratched out his eyes. And from that day, the Prince was blind.

Then he too wandered far into the woods, blindly eating roots and berries, and crying for the loss of his sweet wife. At last, he came to that part of the forest where Rapunzel had made a home among the trees. And by now she had two little children, a boy and a girl who were twins. When the Prince came near, he heard a voice singing which reminded him of his first meeting with Rapunzel, and of all his love and pain since then. He called out so that Rapunzel knew it was him, and she ran into his arms and they wept together.

But by chance, two of her tears fell onto his blind eyes, and suddenly he was cured and could see again. With great joy he took her and his children to his own kingdom. The people ran out to welcome their lost Prince and his family, and they all lived happily for a long time.

The Twelve Brothers

THERE were once a King and a Queen who were happy together and had twelve children, but they were all boys. Then the King said to his wife:

'If our next child is a girl, all the boys must die, so that my daughter may be rich and become Queen of the whole kingdom.'

He had twelve coffins made, with a little pillow in each. Then he locked the coffins in a room, and gave the Queen the key, and told her to keep silent.

The poor mother sat and wept until Benjamin, her youngest son, seeing his mother so sad, asked her why she wept. She could not tell him, but he pressed her with questions, and at last she took him to the locked room, showed him the coffins, and told her son what the King had said.

'Go to the forest with your brothers,' said the Queen, 'and one of you keep a look-out from the highest tree. If I give birth to a son, I'll put a white flag above the tower of the castle, then you may all come back. If I have a daughter, I will hoist a red flag, and then you must all fly away as fast as you can. And I will pray for you, that you may be warm in winter, and that you will not faint in summer.'

When she had blessed her sons, they went into the forest and kept watch in turn. On the twelfth day, when it was Benjamin's turn, he saw a flag being raised. It was a blood-red flag, which meant their death.

Then the brothers were angry. 'Are we to die for a girl?' they cried. 'We will have our revenge. Wherever we find a girl, her red blood shall flow.'

Then they fled deep into the forest and found a little hut, which became their home. They hunted wild animals, and ate the wild fruits and berries. In this way, they lived for ten years.

In the King's palace, the little daughter grew up as good and fair a Princess as you could ever wish to see. On her forehead, she had a golden star. One day, amongst the palace washing, she saw twelve shirts, which were too small for her father. She asked her mother to whom they belonged, and the Queen told her the sad story of her twelve brothers. And with tears in her eyes the Queen took her daughter to the locked room where the coffins stood.

'Dear mother,' said the Princess, 'do not weep, I will go and find my brothers.'

So she took the shirts and went into the deep forest until she came to the little hut. Inside, she found a young lad who was astonished by her beauty, and her royal clothes, and the star on her forehead.

'I am the King's daughter,' she told him, 'and I'm looking for my twelve brothers, and I will go to the ends of the blue sky until I find them.'

Then Benjamin saw that she was his sister, and they kissed and cried together. But Benjamin remembered the brothers' vow to kill all women, so he hid his sister under a tub before the brothers came home from hunting.

That evening, when they were all sitting at supper, Benjamin told them that their sister had arrived. He lifted the tub and the Princess stepped out in all her beauty and glory, with the gold star on her forehead, and the brothers were amazed. They had meant to kill her, but when they saw her they rejoiced and loved her with all their hearts.

Thereafter, the little sister stayed at home with Benjamin. And they looked after the hut and cooked while the eleven elder brothers hunted. And they all lived very happily. One day after supper, as a special treat for her brothers, the Princess plucked twelve lilies from the garden, as a present for the brothers. But the

moment she picked the flowers, the twelve brothers were changed into twelve ravens, which flew away over the forest. And at that same moment, the hut and the garden vanished, leaving the girl alone in the wild woods.

When the Princess looked up, she found an old woman standing by her. The old woman told her that her brothers would be ravens for evermore unless she could do one hard task.

'You must be dumb for seven years,' said the woman, 'and neither speak nor laugh. If in that time, to the last minute, you speak one single word, all will be in vain. This you must do, there is no other way, or else your brothers will die as ravens.'

But the Princess thought in her heart: 'I know I shall set my brothers free.' She found a high tree, and settled herself in it, and spun, and neither spoke nor laughed.

After many days, a King came hunting in the forest. A royal grey-hound broke free from the pack, and seeing the girl in the tree, jumped at her, whining and barking. The King was surprised to find such a beautiful lady in this strange place, with a golden

star on her brow. The more he looked, the more he was captured by her beauty, and at last he asked her to marry him. She spoke no words, but only nodded her head a little.

So the King climbed the tree himself, and carried her down to his horse, and they rode away to the King's palace. They were married without a word, for the bride neither spoke nor laughed, yet they lived happily because they were so glad to be together. But the mother of the King grew jealous of her son's beautiful wife, and since she was a wicked woman, she began to whisper bad things about the young Queen.

'Why, she's nothing but a common beggar that you picked up in the forest,' she told her son. 'Who knows what evil she is thinking? Why can't she speak? Those who don't speak or laugh have wicked thoughts on their mind.'

The King did not want to believe these lies, but his mother nagged at him for so long, and thought up so many bad reasons for the girl's silence, that at last the King believed her, and sentenced his Queen to death.

A great fire was lit in the courtyard, for the Queen to be burnt, and the King stood at the window with tears in his eyes, because he still loved her. The young Queen was fastened to the stake, and the fire began licking at her clothes with its red tongue. But at that very moment, the last minute of her seven year silence came to an end. There was a whirring sound in the air and twelve ravens came plunging out of the sky. And when they touched the earth, they were changed into the twelve brothers whom her silence had saved. They tossed the logs of the fire aside and put out the flames. Then they freed their sister, and hugged her to their hearts and kissed her.

Now at last the Queen could speak. And she opened her mouth and told her husband, the King, why she had been silent and had never laughed. The King wept, and reproached himself bitterly for the terrible way he had treated her. But she forgave him, and the whole family, the King and Queen and her twelve brothers, lived all together happily for many, many years.

But the wicked old step-mother was taken to the judge, who condemned her to death. She was put in a barrel of boiling oil, and died a painful and evil death.

'There's blood on the key,' he said. 'How did it come there?'

Blue-beard

THERE was once a rich man who had lands and houses and fine furniture and horses, and plenty of gold. But he had a blue beard, and this made him so ugly that women ran away from him.

Nearby, in a house owned by a great lady, two beautiful girls were living, and Blue-beard wished that one of them would marry him. But neither would have him. They found him creepy and ugly, and besides he had been married to several other wives, and nobody knew what had happened to them.

So Blue-beard gave a great party, with music and dancing and all kinds of entertainment, and invited the most lively young people in the land. And the two girls were there. The party lasted for eight days, and all the guests had so much fun they forgot to go to bed. Then the younger of the two girls began to think that Blue-beard was not so ugly after all. He was a rich and gallant gentleman, and perhaps she would marry him.

Soon they were married. Some time later, Blue-beard told his wife that he had to visit a far country for many weeks, and that she must see her friends and enjoy herself while he was away.

'Here are the keys to my house and all its treasures,' he said. 'Use what you like. Open the chests that hold my money, my gold and silver. But this little key here is the key to the small room at the end of the gallery, and that room you must not enter. If you do, you shall feel my anger, and there will be great trouble.'

She promised to do what he wished, then he kissed her and left.

As soon as Blue-beard had gone, all the people who were afraid of him came to see his house and to wonder at his riches. His wife showed them the house and the gardens very proudly, and they were amazed.

'All this is very fine,' they said, 'but what's in that little room?'

They kept asking, and soon the wife could not stop her own curiosity. With the key in her trembling hand, she secretly left her guests, went down the back stairs, and opened the little door.

At first, she could see nothing, because the shutters were closed. Then, as her eyes got used to the gloom, she saw that the walls were spattered with red and the floor was sticky with blood. And there, against the wall, were the bodies of several dead women, the wives of Blue-beard who had been murdered and locked in this room.

In her fright, she dropped the key and when she picked it up, it was stained with blood. She fled from the room, and ran with beating heart to her own chamber, where she scrubbed and scrubbed to get the blood off the key. But however much she washed and rubbed, the blood remained.

When Blue-beard returned, his wife tried to seem glad. When he asked for the keys of the house, she shook like a leaf and gave him all but the little key. In a terrible voice, he demanded the little key, and at last she gave it to him.

'There's blood on the key,' he said slowly. 'How did it come there?'

But she said she did not know. She was as pale as death.

'You have opened the door I told you not to,' he replied. 'Very well, madam, you shall take your place among the ladies you saw there.'

She sobbed and begged for mercy, and looked so sad and beautiful she would have melted the heart of a tiger. But Blue-beard was not moved.

'Oh, give me,' she whispered through her sobs, 'time to say my prayers.'

He said he would give her fifteen minutes, and not a moment more.

When she was alone, she called out to her sister:

'Sister, my brothers have promised to come today. Go to the top of the tower and tell them to make haste.'

Her sister climbed the tower, and the poor wife cried:

The house trembled with his anger.

'Sister, sister, do you see them coming?'

But the sister replied:

'I see nothing but the dust dancing in the sun, and the grass growing green.'

Meanwhile, Blue-beard was striding about below, with his sword in his hand, and shouting for his wife to come down and be killed.

'Give me a moment longer,' she begged, and again called out to her sister, 'Sister, do you see them coming?'

And again her sister replied:

'I see nothing but the dust dancing in the sun, and the grass growing green.'

Now Blue-beard was really angry, but his wife called out once more to her sister. And she replied:

'I see a great dust that comes from this side.'

'Are they my brothers?' the poor wife cried in sudden hope.

'Alas, no, my sister dear, all I see is a flock of sheep.'

Then Blue-beard roared again for his wife to come down, but she called out one more desperate time:

'Sister, sister, do you see them coming?'

And now her sister replied:

'I see two horsemen a long way off. And, sister dear, they are our brothers! I have made them a sign to hurry, hurry.'

But now Blue-beard would wait no longer, and the house trembled with his anger. His wife threw herself at his feet, pleading with him to spare her. But he took her by the hair, and raised his sword high, and was about to chop off her head.

At that very moment, there was a loud knock on the gate. Blue-beard stopped. Then the door burst open and the two brothers sprang into the room with their swords ready. Blue-beard let go of his wife and tried to escape. But the young men dashed after him, and caught him on the front steps of the house. They ran their swords through his body and left him dead.

Then the wife was left as the owner of all the lands and all the treasure. She rewarded her sister and her brothers who had saved her, and she gave a decent burial to the sad murdered ladies in the little locked room. At last she was safe, and lived quietly and happily for a long time.

Blue-beard tried to escape, but the young men went after him.

The Tinder Box

A SOLDIER came marching along. One, two! One, two! He had been to the wars, and now he was off home. On the road, he met an old witch, and she was so ugly her lip hung down to her chest.

'Now, here's a *proper* soldier,' said the witch. 'How would you like it if you had all the money you wanted?'

'Much obliged, old witch,' replied the soldier.

So she told him to go to a certain hollow tree and let himself down with a rope around his waist. And there at the bottom would be the money.

'You'll see three doors down there,' she told him. 'In the first room there's a big chest with a dog sitting on it. Don't mind him. He's got eyes as big as teacups, but take my blue-checked apron, put the dog on it, and he'll be as quiet as a lamb. There will be copper coins in that chest, but if you want silver, go to the next room. There's a dog there with eyes as big as millwheels, but just pop him on the apron and take the silver. But maybe you like gold? That's in the third room. The dog there has each eye as big as the Round Tower, he's some dog, I can tell you. But get him on the apron and the gold is yours.'

'That's not bad,' said the soldier, 'but what's in it for you?'

'Not a single penny,' said the witch. 'Just bring me the old tinder box that my granny left behind there.'

So the soldier slid down the tree, and lord help him! there were

'There's a dog there with eyes as big as tea-cups.'

the dogs sure enough. The first two were pretty scary, but that third one, with eyes like Round Towers, why the soldier just had to salute him! But he got the dogs on the apron, and there was enough money to buy the whole of Copenhagen. The soldier filled his knapsack and his pockets and his cap and his boots, and he grabbed the tinder box, and yelled for the witch to pull him up.

'Now you've got the money,' said the witch, 'just give me the tinder box.'

'Fiddlesticks!' said the soldier. 'Tell me straight what the box is for, or I'll cut your head off.'

But she wouldn't tell, so he took his sword and cut her head right off.

With the money and the apron and the tinder box, the soldier went into town and began to live in great style. He looked like a fine gentleman and mixed with all the best people. He heard about the King and the pretty Princess, who was locked up in a copper castle and saw no one, because a magician had said that she would marry an ordinary soldier, and of course the King didn't want that!

'Well, I'd still like to see her,' thought the soldier, but he could not get anywhere near her.

So the soldier lived a merry life, and spent money like water. He even gave a lot to the poor, because he remembered what it had been like when he was poor. And before he knew what had happened, he was suddenly poor again, because he had spent it all. And there he was, in a little attic room, right under the roof, cleaning his own boots, and nobody came to see him anymore.

One evening, when he lacked a match to light his candle, he remembered the tinder box that he had taken from the witch. As soon as he had struck a spark, the door flew open, and in came the dog with eyes like teacups, whom he had seen under the hollow tree.

'What are my lord's orders?' said the dog.

'Oh, it's you, old fellow?' said the soldier. 'How about getting me some money?'

And in a moment the dog was back with a great bag of copper coins in his mouth.

Well, the soldier saw what a lovely tinder box this was. If he struck it once, the dog from the copper room came. If he struck it twice, he saw the dog with the silver. And three times, there was the dog with the gold. Now the soldier was back in business. He got some more smart clothes, and scattered money around town, and soon everyone was fond of him again.

Then the soldier got to thinking about that poor Princess, all locked away in the castle. So he gave the tinder box a rub and in came the dog with the teacup eyes.

'I know it's the middle of the night,' he said, 'but I'd certainly like to see the Princess.'

And in a minute the dog was back with the sleeping Princess. She looked so pretty, and every inch a Princess, that the soldier just had to give her a kiss, because that was a soldierly thing to do. And then the dog took her back to the castle.

Next morning, at breakfast, the Princess said she'd had a funny dream. There had been a dog and a soldier. The great big dog had given her a ride on his back, and the soldier had kissed her.

'My word,' said the Queen, 'that's a strange story.' And she told one of her ladies to keep a good watch on the Princess's bed, just to make sure she really was dreaming.

Now the next night, the dog came again for the Princess, and the lady-in-waiting raced after them. At the soldier's house, she put a large chalk cross on the door, to mark it. But the dog saw what she had done, and marked a cross on every other door in the street, so that the King and Queen could not find the soldier's house.

But the Queen was a clever woman who knew a trick or two herself. She took her golden scissors and a piece of silk and made a

The great big dog carried her on his back.

bag with a tiny hole in it. Then she filled the bag with flour and tied it to the nightdress of the sleeping Princess. When the dog came, and carried the Princess off to the soldier, the flour trickled from the bag all the way to the soldier's house.

And then the game was up. The King came next day with his guards and slammed the soldier in the dungeon. He was going to be hanged in the morning, and he didn't even have his tinder box on him!

Next morning, when everyone was rushing by to get a good position at the hanging, the soldier called out to a shoemaker's boy:

'Hey, little man, don't be in such a hurry. Nothing is going to happen until I get there! If you go to my house and fetch my tinder box, I'll give you fourpence.'

So the boy dashed to the house and back, and gave the soldier the tinder box.

Outside the town, the gallows had been built, and the King and the Queen and just about everyone else were there waiting. As the soldier was led up the ladder with a rope around his neck, he asked if he could have one last wish. He would dearly like to smoke one more pipe of tobacco. The King didn't mind, so the soldier took out his tinder box, to light his pipe, and struck it three times. One, two, three! And there were all the dogs! The one with eyes like teacups, the one with eyes like millwheels, and the monster fellow with each eye like a Round Tower.

'Help me now,' cried the soldier, and the dogs took the judges and the gentlemen and the guards by the arm or the leg or the nose and tossed them away. And the biggest dog took the King and the Queen too, and threw them after the rest.

Then all the people were frightened and called out:

'Dear soldier, dear good solider, be kind and you shall be our King and have the lovely Princess for your wife.'

Then the soldier got in the King's coach, and the dogs galloped in front, and the boys whistled through their fingers, and the guards saluted. The Princess was led out of the copper castle and made Queen, and very pleased she was too. The wedding lasted eight days, and the whole town had a great time, and the dogs sat at the wedding table goggling with their great big cheerful eyes.

Snow White

IT was winter, and the Queen was sewing by the window, looking through the black ebony frame at the falling snow. As she sewed, she pricked her finger, and three drops of blood fell on the unmarked snow. She gazed at the spots of bright red blood and thought:

'I wish my daughter to be as white as snow, as red as blood, as black as ebony.'

And so it was. The Queen's daughter grew into a girl with skin as white as snow, with lips as red as blood, and with hair as black as ebony. And she was called Snow White.

Then the Queen died, and the King married another wife who was very beautiful but very, very cold. She could not bear to think that anyone was more beautiful than she was. Many times, she looked in her magic mirror and said:

> Mirror, mirror, tell me true,
> Of all the ladies in the land,
> Who is the fairest, tell me who?

And the mirror answered:

> *You are the fairest in the land.*

But Snow White was growing up and becoming more and more lovely, and one day, when the Queen went to her mirror, the mirror replied:

She came upon a strange little cottage and went in to rest.

Listen, Queen, what I tell you is true,
Snow White is lovelier far than you!

Then the Queen turned pale from anger and envy. She sent a servant to take Snow White away to some place where the child would never be seen again. The servant knew he was meant to kill the little girl, but he could not do it. So he left her in the forest, at the mercy of the weather and the beasts.

Snow White wandered through that wild land in great fear. At last, worn out but unharmed, she came to a strange little cottage and went in to rest. Inside, everything was very neat and small. On the table were seven little places with seven little plates and seven little loaves and seven little glasses of wine. By the wall stood seven little beds. As Snow White was hungry, she took a nibble from each loaf and drank a drop from each glass. Then she felt tired, so she tried the beds until she found one just her size. She snuggled under the bed-clothes and went fast asleep.

Presently, in marched seven little dwarfs, returning home from the day's work, which was digging for gold in the mountains. As they lit their lamps, they saw that everything was not right.

'Who's been sitting on my stool?' said the first.

'Who's been eating from my plate?' said the second.

'Who's been picking at my bread?' said the third.

'Who's been using my spoon?' said the fourth.

'Who's been meddling with my fork?' said the fifth.

'Who's been cutting with my knife?' said the sixth.

'Who's been drinking from my glass?' said the seventh.

And the first one, who had been looking around the little house, added:

'And who's *that* lying in my bed?'

They gathered around in amazement, and when they lifted their lamps to take a good look and saw how peacefully Snow White was sleeping, they let her sleep on. The dwarfs were kind little fellows, and to tell the truth they felt rather pleased to have such a pretty visitor.

Next morning, Snow White told them her story, and they took pity on her. They offered to let her stay. They were busy little men, out all day looking for gold, and they thought she would be useful in the house, to cook and wash and keep them tidy. But they warned her: 'Take care of the Queen. She will learn you are not dead and will come looking for you. When we are out, let no one in.'

For a while, the Queen was happy. But one day, as she questioned her mirror, the answer gave her a nasty shock:

You, O Queen, are the fairest here,
But over the hills, in the greenwood shade,
Where seven dwarfs their house have made,
There Snow White is hiding from you, and she
Is lovelier far than you'll ever be!

The Queen knew that the mirror never lied. She felt a terrible jealousy. And since her servant had tricked her, she decided to get rid of Snow White herself. In disguise, she went over the mountains to the place where the dwarfs lived. She knocked at the door, crying: 'Fine things to sell. Laces, cottons, buttons, silk. Buy my pretty things.'

Now, Snow White was very tempted by bright colours and pretty shapes. Surely, she thought, there can be no harm in this old woman. She opened the door.

'Bless me!' said the old woman, entering quickly, 'how badly your dress is laced. Let me take one of my nice new laces and lace you up properly.'

So the Queen in disguise pulled and pulled until Snow White fainted, and down she fell as if dead.

'That's the end of you,' cried the cruel Queen, and away she went.

That evening, when the little men returned, they saw Snow White lying on the floor, and they feared for her. But she was still breathing, so they cut her laces and rubbed and bathed her, and soon she was well again. 'Be careful,' they anxiously warned her once more. 'That old woman was really the wicked Queen. Never, never open the door when we are away.'

As soon as the Queen got home she went straight to the mirror. But the mirror answered as before:

Still Snow White is hiding from you, and she
Is lovelier far than ever you'll be!

Now the Queen was raging with envy. Again, she put on a

E CANNOT LAY HER IN THE DARK EARTH" SAID THE DWARFS AND SO THEY HAD A TRANSPARENT GLASS COFFIN MADE SO THAT SHE COULD BE SEEN FROM EVERY SIDE LAID HER IN IT AND WROTE ON IT HER NAME AND THAT SHE WAS A KINGS DAUGHTER THEN THEY CARRIED THE COFFIN INTO THE WOOD AND SOME OF THEM ALWAYS WATCHED HER AND THE BIRDS ALSO CAME AND BEWAILED SNOWDROP FIRST AN OWL THEN A RAVEN AND LASTLY A DOVE SO SNOWDROP LAY A LONG LONG TIME IN HER COFFIN LOOKING AS THOUGH SHE WERE ASLEEP.

They laid her in a coffin of glass.

disguise and hurried over the mountains. This time she was selling combs, one of which she had poisoned. And again Snow White, tempted by pretty things, let her in. At once, the wicked Queen put the poisoned comb in Snow White's hair, to eat into her brain, and went away glad.

Luckily, the seven dwarfs returned early that day. Seeing what was wrong, they quickly pulled the comb from her hair and rubbed her head with a special medicine that made Snow White recover.

The Queen was now sure that Snow White was dead, but again the mirror told her otherwise. Pale with anger and determined to kill her this time, the Queen took a rosy apple and poisoned half of it. Then she knocked again at the dwarfs' door, dressed as an old peasant woman. But Snow White would not let her in.

'Silly girl,' said the Queen. 'I've brought you a lovely apple. Take it.

But Snow White would not take it.

'Are you afraid it's poisoned?' mocked the Queen. 'Look, I'll cut it in half, then I'll eat one half and you the other.'

Well, surely that was safe, Snow White thought. So she reached from the window and took the poisoned half and ate it, and fell down dead.

'Nothing will save you this time,' cried the Queen, and went home to her mirror, which said at last:

Now you are the fairest of all the fair.

The cruel face of the Queen broke into a smile of happiness.

When they returned that night, the seven dwarfs found Snow White lying without breath or movement. She seemed quite dead. So they bathed her with wine mixed with water. Then they laid her on a bed and watched and wept for three days. They could not bear to put her in the cold ground, so they made a coffin of glass, where all could see her beauty, and wrote her name in golden letters. They placed the coffin on a hill, with one of the dwarfs always by it, to keep it guarded. And even the birds came to see her and to mourn. First came an owl, then a raven, and then a dove.

Thus Snow White lay in her glass coffin for a long time, looking as white as snow, as red as blood, as black as ebony. After many years a prince rode by. When he had seen the coffin and read the golden letters, he begged the little men to let him take her away, and he offered them all the money they wished. But the dwarfs replied:

'Though we would not sell her for all the gold in the world, we will let you take her out of pity.'

Then, as the Prince lifted Snow White from the coffiin, to carry her home, the piece of apple fell from her throat, and she awoke.

'Where am I?' she whispered, as if waking from a long bad dream.

'You are safe with me,' said the Prince softly. And so she was. And soon after they agreed to get married.

Invitations to the marriage went out to all the royal courts of the nearby lands. And among them was an invitation to the cruel

Queen. She got out her finest clothes, and when she was dressed she looked at herself proudly in the magic mirror. And once more she asked:

> Mirror, mirror, tell me true,
> Of all the ladies in the land,
> Who is fairest, tell me who?

And the mirror, which could not lie, answered:

> *Here, you are the loveliest seen,*
> *But lovelier far is the new-made Queen.*

In surprise and anger, fearing what she might find, the cruel Queen journeyed to the far palace for the wedding. And when she saw that the new-made Queen was indeed Snow White, alive and more beautiful than ever, she fell ill and died of rage and spite.

But Snow White and her Prince lived and ruled happily for many a long year.

The King of the Golden Mountain

THERE was once a merchant who had two children. He was a rich man, with two ships, but on a certain journey both his ships sank, with all his goods, and then he was poor, having nothing left but a single field.

One day, he was walking in this field, full of sad thoughts, when a strange little black man appeared and offered to help him.

'Forget your troubles,' said the dwarf. 'Promise to give me the first thing that rubs against your leg at home, and to bring it to me here in twelve years, and then you shall have as much money as you like.'

The merchant thought, 'Why, that must be my dog,' and forgot all about his little boy. So he said yes to the little black man, and wrote out his promise and went home.

As he entered the door, his small son trotted up and caught him fast by the leg. With a shock, the father remembered his promise and did not know what to do. Perhaps the dwarf was joking? But then, looking for some old things to sell in the attic, the merchant found a great heap of money. He knew now that the dwarf had spoken truly, but because he had money again, he soon forgot the dwarf and began to live like a great merchant.

The boy grew up tall and handsome and clever. As the twelfth year came closer, the merchant remembered his promise, and he grew sad. His son asked him what was wrong, and at last the merchant told him of the promise.

'Don't worry, father,' said the son, 'the black dwarf has no power over me.'

When the time came, after twelve years, father and son went to the field, drew a large circle and stepped inside it. The dwarf came to claim what was his, but the son, who had been blessed by the priest, defied the little man, and would not go. They argued for some time and then agreed that the son now belonged to neither the father nor the dwarf. There was a river flowing nearby, and the black dwarf said that the son must put himself in a boat, and the father must push it off with his own foot. When this was done, the boat tipped over, and the father, believing that his son was lost, went home and mourned.

But the boat did not sink and the youth was safe inside it. At last, he landed on an unknown shore and saw a fine castle. But when he got to it, he found it was bewitched. He walked through empty rooms until he came to the last, where a huge snake lay coiled in a ring. The snake called out to him, and said she was really a maiden under a magic spell, and she welcomed him as the person to set her free.

'But how shall I do that?' he asked.

'Twelve black dwarfs,' she answered, 'will come tonight and question you. Be silent, and let them do what they will with you. If they beat you or torture you, say not a word, and at midnight they will go. On the second night, twelve more will come, and on the third night, twenty-four. They will cut off your head, but at midnight they will lose their power, and if you have done as I say, I shall be free. Then I will come with the water of life, and rub you with it, and make you whole and healthy again.

It happened just as she said. After the third night, the snake became a Princess again. She cured the young man with the magic water, and then she kissed him. The next day she married him, to the great joy of all the people around the castle, and he became the King of the Golden Mountain.

For eight years they lived happily, and the Queen gave birth to a fine boy. Then the King remembered his father, and he wished to visit him. But the Queen was afraid, and said:

'I know your visit will bring me unhappiness.'

As the King was determined to go, the Queen let him leave, giving him for his travels a magic wishing-ring which he could use for any purpose, except he must not wish the Queen to leave the castle.

The King turned the ring, and in a moment he was outside the town where his father lived. But he was dressed so richly and strangely that the guards turned him back from the gate. Then he went to the fields and changed his clothes for those of a shepherd, and went to his father's house. But the merchant thought that his son was long dead and would not recognize him.

'Our son,' said the merchant, 'has a strawberry mark under the right arm.'

So the young man took off his shirt and showed his father the mark, and told him that he was the King of the Golden Mountain, and was married to a Princess, and they had a fine son seven years old.

'Surely this is a lie,' the father said again. 'It's a strange sort of King who goes about in a ragged shepherd's coat.'

Then the son was angry and, without thinking of his promise, he turned the ring and wished his wife and child to be there. They arrived at once, but the Queen was weeping, because he had broken his word. He tried to calm her, saying that he had merely been thoughtless. But she did not forgive him.

He took her to the field outside the town and showed her the place on the river from which the boat had pushed off. Then he said he was tired and lay down to sleep in her lap. As he slept, she gently took the ring from his finger, lifted his head from her lap, and left only her slipper. Then she took her child and wished herself back in her own castle.

When he awoke, he lay alone, in ragged clothes, in an empty field. He was ashamed to return to his father, so he set off to walk to his own wife and his own kingdom.

As he walked, he saw three giants arguing about things their father had left them. The giants called to him, to help them divide their property, because they thought that little men had quick wits. They had been left three things. The first was a sword which would obey the order 'All heads off but mine.' The second was a cloak that made one invisible. And the third was a pair of magic boots that could whisk one away in a moment.

The King of the Golden Mountain asked to see these three things. He tried the invisible cloak, and it was good. He tried the sword, but only against the trees, and it cut them in half. Then he asked for the boots, but the giants said:

'No, if we give you the boots, you will fly away over the hill with our things, and then we will have nothing.'

He said he would not do this, so the giants gave him the boots also.

But as he put them on, he could think only of his wife and child, and he could not help saying to himself:

'Oh, if only I were back on the Golden Mountain.'

At once, the boots carried him away, and he vanished from the sight of the giants, and so their property was divided from them after all.

As he landed near his castle, he heard sounds of joy, with fiddles and flutes and dancing, and the people told him that his Queen was marrying another man. Then he was angry.

'This is the false woman,' he thought, 'who left me while I slept, and now she betrays me with another man!'

So he put on the giants' cloak and went, quite invisible, into the castle. There was a feast on the table, and the guests were eating and drinking and laughing. The woman who had been his wife sat on the throne with a crown on her head. He went behind her, still invisible, and when she took a piece of meat, he ate it, and when she poured some wine, he drank it, so she had nothing.

This made her afraid, so she rose from the feast, ran to her room and wept. But he followed her.

'All heads off but mine!'

'Am I still in the devil's power?' she cried. 'Did the man who changed me from a snake never come?'

Then he hit her across the face, saying:

'I am the man who saved you, and I have you in my power, you traitor. Have I deserved this from you?'

Now he took off the cloak and made himself visible again. He left the Queen weeping and returned to the feast.

'The wedding is at an end,' he cried, 'the true King has come back!'

But all the Kings and Princes and great lords looked at him as if he were a fool, and they mocked him. So he said to them all:

'Will you leave, or not?'

Then they were outraged, and they rushed towards him and tried to seize him. At once, he drew the giants' magic sword, and cried:

'All heads off but mine!'

The sword snicked through the air, and all the heads rolled on the ground. In a moment, he was alone, the lord of the castle, and once more King of the Golden Mountain.

Beauty and the Beast

IN a far country, there was a merchant who had once been rich, but fell on hard times. His children, used to the best things, did not like their new life in a poor cottage. They had grown selfish and spoilt, and they complained bitterly. All except one.

She was the youngest, and she was neither selfish not spoilt. In their little cottage she did the housework while the others complained. And because she was so willing and kind and pretty her father called her Beauty.

Then the merchant heard that a ship which he had thought was lost had now returned. Thinking that his fortune was saved, he prepared to go to the city and asked the children, just as he used to do, what presents he could bring them. The brothers and sisters wanted many expensive and foolish things, but Beauty asked for no present, except to see her father safe home.

'O, do accept something,' her father said. And at last she asked for just one rose.

In the city, the arrival of the lost ship led to bitter arguments. The quarrel was taken to court, but after six months, while the lawyers grew rich, nothing was settled. In mid-winter, the merchant sadly set out for home, as poor as he had ever been. As he went, the snow was falling. In the gloom of the forest he could not find the path and the wolves howled. His horse stumbled, blinded by the weather.

In the night, the merchant almost gave up hope, for it seemed that death was coming to gather him. But next morning, suddenly he found himself in a strange land of sunlight. Instead of snow-covered forest paths he saw an avenue of orange-trees leading through gardens to a castle with towers that reached into the sky. He rode to the door and called but there was no answer. He stabled his horse and entered the castle, going through rooms full of light and treasures and silence. In a far room he found food ready. Then, tired out by his journey, he slept.

When he awoke he was still alone. In the great, silent rooms he could find no one. He walked through the castle and through the gardens, seeing wonderful things on every side, and soon he began to think of his lost wealth and of his family. How happy they would be in this place! And since there seemed to be no one here, why should he not fetch them? Yes, he would do it. So he hurried to the stables, but as he passed through a pathway of roses he remembered his promise to his youngest, dearest child. He stopped and picked a single red rose.

At once, there was a terrible noise and a monstrous Beast stood in the path.

'Did I not,' the frightful thing roared, 'give you the freedom of my castle? How dare you steal my rose. I have a mind to kill you right now.'

The merchant fell on his knees, begging for mercy. He explained his sad story, telling the Beast that the rose was for his daughter Beauty who was so good and kind. The Beast listened, grinding his ugly teeth. But when he spoke again he was not quite so fierce.

'Your life will be saved,' said the Beast, 'if one of your daughters will offer to live with me here. Go now, and let them choose. Return at the end of the month. And do not think you can escape my power.'

The horse seemed to know the way without any guide, but the merchant rode with a heavy heart. At the cottage, his children, who had feared that their father was dead, kissed him and laughed with joy. But when they heard what the Beast had said they were angry and blamed Beauty for wanting the rose. Now they would have to fly to a far land, beyond the reach of the Beast.

But Beauty said: 'Dear father, it is my fault. Come, let us go to the castle. I will stay with the Beast.'

Every evening, at supper, the beast came.

Sadly the merchant agreed, and sadly they returned to the strange castle, standing above the forest so shining and mysterious. They went through the rich, empty rooms and again found a meal made ready. When they were eating they heard a roaring of wind. The door burst open and the Beast came in like thunder.

'Well, Beauty,' he bellowed, 'have you chosen to stay?'

His looks were terrible to her eyes, but she answered quietly that she would stay.

'Very well, but your father must leave. He may take two trunks of jewels for his family but he must never return. Choose what you like, then wave your father goodbye.'

With many tears she kissed her father goodbye. Then, worn out by sorrow, and by fear for the future, she fell on her bed and slept. She dreamed. She found herself in a golden country of meadows and woods. As she wandered there a handsome Prince appeared and spoke to her in a tender and loving way, begging her to be kind to him.

'Dear Prince,' she sighed, 'what can I do to help you?'

'Be grateful for what you are given,' he replied, 'but do not believe all you see. Above all, do not leave me. Rescue me from my cruel suffering.'

Then the Prince faded away and his place in the dream was taken by a tall, lovely lady, who commanded Beauty: 'Do not sigh for the past. Have faith and do not believe in appearances only. Great things await you in the future.'

Thus began her life in the castle. Each day, she wandered through the rooms and the gardens. She met no one. Hidden hands prepared everything she might need. The days sped by with music and magical entertainments. And every evening, at supper, the Beast came, snorting and twisting his ugly great head.

'Well, Beauty,' he roared, 'are you going to marry me?'

But Beauty shook with fright and tried to creep away. And when the Beast had gone she went quickly to bed and entered the land of dreams where her Prince was waiting.

'Do not be so cruel,' the Prince would beg. 'I love you but you are so stubborn. Help me out of my misery.' He had a crown in his hands, which he offered her, kneeling and weeping at her feet.

But what did this dreaming mean? Beauty did not know. Her days were full of wonders. The sun shone always, and the birds sang. Bands of pretty apes were her servants. But each evening came the Beast, with his grim looks and his terrible question. And each night, in sleep, her Prince sighed for his freedom.

As the days passed, slowly she began to feel sorry for the Beast. He was kind, in his rough way, and gave her everything. Surely his ugliness was not his fault. But she was lonely, too. She saw no one but the Beast. She missed her family. She began to sleep badly. Her dreams were full of worry. Her Prince seemed close to despair.

Then, one night, she dreamed that the Prince ran at the Beast with a dagger, meaning to kill him. Beauty stepped between them, pleading for the Beast, saying that the terrible monster was her friend and protector. The Prince disappeared and at once the tall lady was standing in his place.

'You will soon be happy,' she told Beauty, 'but only if you do not believe in appearances.'

Next morning, waking tired and sad and lonely, she decided to ask the Beast for permission to see her family just once more.

When the Beast heard this he fell to the ground and groaned. But he said he could not deny anything to his Beauty. She could go, and take four chests of treasure with her. But if she did not return after two months, her Beast would die.

Her family were amazed to see her. Her father laughed and cried to have his favourite daughter back. And the four chests of treasure made even her brothers and sisters forget their troubles. They all begged her not to go back to the castle, and for a while she was so happy with her family that she never thought of the Beast.

Two months went by without her notice. Then, one night, she had another dream. She dreamed that she saw the Beast at the point of death. At once, she awoke. She remembered a ring that the Beast had given her, and turning it on her finger she was carried in a flash to the castle. She ran through the great, silent rooms but there was no sign of the monster. She dashed into the gardens and the park, calling his name, running here and there. At last, when night had fallen, she stumbled on his still body in the moonlight.

'Dear Beast,' she cried, 'are you dead? O, please forgive me. I never realized before that I love you. Now I fear I have killed you.'

Her presence began to revive him.

Before her stood the Prince of her dreams.

But his heart was still beating and her presence began to revive him. In a while he was able to stagger to the castle. As he lay on a sofa, she heard him whisper in his sad, growling voice.

'Beauty, have you come back to me? Will you marry me now?'

And she answered at once: 'Yes, dear Beast.'

Then there was a blaze of lights, and loud music, and the Beast vanished. Instead, before her stood the Prince of her dreams, with the tall lady beside him. Beauty and the Prince took hands, and the lady smiled and blessed them.

'You have rescued my son,' she told Beauty, 'from the evil magic that has imprisoned him for so long in the hideous body of the Beast. When you chose him freely, you released the Prince from the spell. Now you will marry him. No longer will you be Beauty and the Beast, but the Prince and Princess of all this great and lovely land.'

The Garden of Paradise

THERE was once a King's son who had ever so many books, but none of them could tell him where to find the Garden of Paradise, which was what he wanted to know most of all.

Years ago, his Granny had told him that flowers in the Garden of Paradise tasted like delicious cake, and that their nectar tasted like wine. History grew in the Garden like a plant, and so did geography and languages, and every time you took a nibble you learned more and more. At first, the boy believed this. But as he grew older he realized that the Garden of Paradise must be far stranger and finer than that.

'Oh, why,' he thought, 'did Adam and Eve take and eat the forbidden fruit from the Tree of Knowledge? If only I'd been there, it wouldn't have happened. Then there would be no sin in the world.'

For years, he thought about this. The Garden of Paradise was in his mind most of the time.

One day, lost and wet in the forest, the Prince came to a huge cave, with a fire burning inside and the smell of roast stag coming from it. An elderly woman, tall and strong as a man in disguise, welcomed him to the fire to dry his clothes. The Prince huddled up to the flames, but he still complained of a strong draught that whipped through the cave.

'That's nothing,' said the woman. 'Wait till my sons come home. For this is the Cave of the Winds, and my sons are the Four Winds

He found himself already high above the clouds.

of the World. They're wild fellows and do as they please. They're out in the skies now, playing bat and ball with the clouds.'

'Well,' replied the Prince, 'this is a rough place, and you seem to be a hard old woman.'

'That's right,' she said. 'But I have to be harsh, to control my boys, who are pretty obstinate lads. Sometimes I have to pick them up and push them into those sacks by the wall. They fear that, I can tell you, just as you fear the birch-rod behind the looking-glass.'

Just then, the North Wind came howling in, with hail and snow around him, and icicles hanging from his beard. He had come from Arctic seas and lands of ice, where the bones of whales looked like a giant's arms covered in green mould. He had seen the hunted walrus shaking his long tusks below the waves. He had seen blood spurt from harpoon wounds, and he had roared among the hunters and battered their boats with storms.

'Oh, you've been up to mischief!' said the mother of the winds.

At this moment, in came the West Wind, looking like a wild man, with a padded hat, and a mahogany club from the American forests. He came from the wilderness, where there were no men, and water-snakes rested in the damp grass. He had raised such a storm that the river carried away the wading buffalo, and great trees crashed to the ground. Ah, he was a fierce fellow, and he kissed his mother so roughly that she almost fell over.

Next came the South Wind, wearing a turban and wrapped up like a Bedouin. But he complained of the cold, and threw more wood on the fire. He had come from Africa, where the plains were as green as olives, and the wind ran races with deer and ostrich. In the desert, he had spun the loose sand into dancing pillars and covered over the thirsty caravan, so that men and animals would die and the sun bleach their bones.

'That's bad,' cried the mother. 'Into the sack you go!' And she grabbed the South Wind, forced him into a sack, and sat on him to keep him quiet.

'Surely these are desperate fellows,' said the Prince.

'Yes, indeed,' she replied, 'but I can deal with them. And here comes the last of them. Well, my East Wind, I thought you were going to the Garden of Paradise?'

The East Wind, who was dressed in Chinese style, said he was

They were in a land of music and beautiful maidens.

going to the Garden tomorrow. He had just come from China, where he had seen officials flogged for their own good. He had rushed through belfries and towers, making bells sing, 'tsing, tsang, tsu'.

'You're a wild one,' laughed his mother. 'Just as well you're off to the Garden of Paradise. That always makes you behave better. Remember to take a deep drink from the fount of wisdom, and bring a little bottleful for me.'

When the East Wind saw his brother in the sack, he pleaded with his mother and gave her some fresh green China tea to release her naughty son. Ashamed, the South Wind crept from the sack. Then they all sat down to eat roast stag, and the Prince began to ask the East Wind about the Garden of Paradise.

'Ah,' said the East Wind, 'why not come with me tomorrow? But I must warn you that no human has been there since Adam and Eve. After they were driven out, the Garden sank under the earth. The Queen of the Fairies lives there, and there too is the Island of Bliss, where death never comes. Sit on my back tomorrow, but now we must sleep.'

When the Prince awoke the next morning, he found himself already high above the clouds, clinging to the back of the East Wind, while the country whirled by like a coloured map.

'Good morning,' cried the East Wind. 'Sleep longer if you like. There's little to see here, unless you like counting church spires.'

They swept on, flying over the world, faster than eagles or horses. In the evening, the Prince clapped his hands at the lights twinkling like sparks among the houses of the towns. But the East Wind told him to hold on tight. Turning south, they passed the Himalayas and began to smell a land of fruit and fragrant spices. Then they dropped down to a meadow where flowers nodded a welcome to the East Wind.

'Nearly there,' said the Wind. 'Do you see that cave, with a vine in front like a green curtain? Wrap your cloak around you. One step into that cave is as cold as ice, but that's the way we must go.'

Oh, how cold it was! 'Surely this is the road to Death,' thought the Prince. But they passed through the cavern into a world of blue light and soft air, as fresh as a stream and as sweet-smelling as a rose. A marble bridge crossed a river in which gold and silver fishes

This was the Fairy Princess of the Garden.

played, and little electric-blue sparks shot from purple eels. The East Wind carried the Prince over the bridge, into the Garden of Paradise.

Then they were in a land of flowers and music and beautiful maidens. Peacocks spread their tails among the palm trees, and birds as bright as paint glittered in the foliage. Tame animals stood in the fields. The lion lay with the antelope, and shy wood-pigeons fluttered around the tiger's head.

A beautiful young woman approached. Her face was as calm and radiant as the summer sun. This was the Fairy Princess of the Garden of Paradise. Taking the Prince by the hand, she led him to her palace, where the living pictures of Time were displayed, like a stage-show, in panes of glass. The Prince witnessed the temptation of Adam and Eve. He saw the dream of Jacob's ladder, and many other wonderful events, all shown in the glass windows.

They came to the innermost hall of the palace, and there, among portraits of the blessed who smiled and sang, stood a tree with golden apples. This was the Tree of Knowledge. A drop of bright red dew hung from every leaf, as if the tree were weeping tears of blood.

Then the Fairy took the Prince to a boat, which rocked gently on the water, but did not move. Yet all the lands of the earth came gliding by, with all their mountains and valleys and forests, all their strange animals, their bright and dark places, their wonders and mysteries.

'May I stay here forever?' begged the Prince in delight.

'That depends on you,' answered the Fairy. 'Adam disobeyed the rules, but if you can keep them you may stay.'

'But I'll never touch the apple of the Tree of Knowledge,' cried the Prince.

'Think carefully,' said the Fairy. 'The East Wind will not return for a hundred years. That's a long time for temptation and sin. Every evening I shall tempt you to come with me. But beware of my call! Do not follow, for I'll be calling you to the hall with the Tree of Knowledge. I shall sleep under its branches. You will be tempted to touch me, but if you do, Paradise will vanish from you. A sharp wind will whistle for you, icy rain will drip from your hair, and sorrow will be your inheritance.'

'I shall stay,' cried the Prince. Then the East Wind spread his great wings, kissed the Prince on the forehead, and flew away crying, 'Farewell, farewell, for a hundred years.'

When the Wind had gone, the Fairy led the Prince to a hall of white lilies. Inside the flowers were yellow stamens in the form of golden harps which made a clear, sweet music. As the setting sun turned the sky pure gold, they danced and they danced. Then the walls drew back and the Prince saw the Tree of Knowledge dazzling his eyes. And he heard a soft voice singing, 'My darling, my beloved, my darling child.'

The Fairy left him and began to beckon, saying 'Come with me, oh come with me.' And the Prince immediately ran towards her, forgetting his promise even on this very first evening.

There was a fragrant smell in the air, and the harps made his head ring so sweetly, and in the hall with the Tree the portraits nodded and sang, 'We must know everything. Man is the lord of the earth.' Instead of the tears of blood, red stars seemed to drop from the leaves of the Tree.

The Fairy called the Prince forward. In the innermost hall, she took off her shimmering clothes, parted the branches of the Tree, and was hidden beneath them.

'I've not sinned yet,' thought the Prince, 'nor will I.'

But he drew back the branches and saw her sleeping, with tears trembling behind her eyelids.

'Don't weep, lovely maiden,' whispered the Prince. And he kissed the tears from her eyes.

At once, there was a clap of thunder. The Fairy vanished, and Paradise sank into the earth. A terrible cold shot through the limbs of the Prince, and he fell with closed eyes, as if dead. When he came to, a bitter rain was beating on his face and a sharp wind pierced him through.

'What have I done?' he moaned. 'I have sinned like Adam, and Paradise is lost to me.' He looked up and saw the morning star sparkling in the heavens like his lost land. Then he rose, and he found himself by the Cave of the Winds, with the mother of the winds glaring at him angrily.

'The very first evening!' she cried. 'Well, I expected it. If you were my son, I'd put you straight in a sack.'

'And that's where he'll go,' said Death standing by. He was a strong old man, with a scythe and black wings.

'He'll die all right,' Death continued, 'but not yet. First I'll see if he repents. He may grow to be good. But I'll come back one secret day and lay him in my black coffin. If he's still full of sin, he'll sink like the lost Garden. But if he's good, I'll put the coffin on my head and fly to the stars, where he shall live and sparkle forever.'

The Frog Prince

ONE fine evening, a young Princess went to play, down by the cool spring. She threw her golden ball up and down, up and down, but then she missed her catch, and the golden ball rolled into the spring. The Princess looked into the water, but it was so deep she could not see the bottom. She began to cry:

'Alas, if I could only get my ball I'd give all my fine clothes and all my jewels, and everything I have in the world.'

A frog popped his head out of the water.

'Princess,' he said, 'why are you weeping so bitterly?'

'My golden ball,' she answered, 'has fallen in the spring. But what can you do for me, you nasty frog?'

Then the frog said: 'Keep your pearls and jewels and fine clothes. But if you will love me, and let me live with you and eat from your golden plate, and sleep upon your bed, I will bring you your ball.'

'What nonsense!' thought the Princess. 'This silly frog can't even leave the spring. But he could get my ball, so I might as well tell him he can have what he asks.'

Then she said to the frog: 'Well, bring me my ball and I'll do all you ask.'

The frog dived deep under the water and came up with the ball in his mouth, and threw it on the bank by the edge of the spring. When the young Princess saw the golden ball, she was full of joy. She picked it up and began to run home without another thought for the frog. The frog called after her:

'Stop, Princess. Remember your promise. Take me with you.'
But the Princess ran on and did not hear a word.

Next day, just as the Princess sat down to dinner, she heard a strange noise – a tapping and a splashing – as if something rather wet was coming up the marble stairs. There was a gentle knock at the door and a little voice said:

'Open the door, my Princess dear,
Open the door to thy true love here!
And mind the words that thou and I said
By the fountain cool in the greenwood shade.'

The Princess opened the door and saw the frog, whom she had quite forgotten. She was sadly frightened, and shut the door as fast as she could. Her father, the King, seeing that she was scared, asked her what was wrong.

'There's a nasty frog at the door,' she said. 'He fetched me my ball from the spring, and I told him he could live with me, thinking that he could never get out of the water. But here he is at the door, and he wants to come in!'

And while she was speaking, there was another little knock and the quiet voice said:

'Open the door, my Princess dear,
Open the door to thy true love here!
And mind the words that thou and I said
By the fountain cool in the greenwood shade.'

The King said to the young Princess:
'You've given your word and now you must keep it. Go and let him in.' The frog hopped into the room and came close to the table where the Princess sat.

'Pray lift me up,' he said to her, 'and let me sit next to you.' And when she had done this, the frog said:

'Put your plate near to me, so I may eat out of it.'

She did this, and when he had eaten as much as he could, he said:
'Now I'm tired. Carry me upstairs and put me in your bed.'

And very unwillingly the Princess took him in her hand, and placed him on the pillow of her own bed, where he slept all night.

As soon as it was day, the frog jumped up, hopped downstairs, and was gone.

'He's gone at last,' thought the Princess. 'I'll have no more trouble from him.'

But she was wrong. When night came, she heard the same tapping at the door, and the same little voice:

'Open the door, my Princess dear,
Open the door to thy true love here!
And mind the words that thou and I said
By the fountain cool in the greenwood shade.'

And the frog came in, and slept on her pillow as before, and left in the morning. And on the third night he did the same. But when the Princess awoke on the following morning, she was amazed to see, instead of the frog, a handsome Prince with beautiful eyes standing by the head of the bed.

He told her that he had been changed into a frog by a wicked fairy. And he had to live in the spring as a frog until some Princess would take him out, and let him eat from her plate, and sleep on her bed for three nights.

'You,' said the Prince, 'have broken the cruel charm at last. Now let us go to my father's kingdom, where I will marry you, and love you as long as you live.'

You may be sure that the Princess quickly agreed to this. And soon a beautiful coach drove up, with eight fine horses, with plumes and feathers and golden harness. And behind the coach was the Prince's faithful servant, who had wept so bitterly for his dear master during all the long years of his enchantment.

Then full of joy they got into the coach, and the horses sprang forward towards the Prince's land. They arrived safely and lived there a great many happy years.

Index of Artists

Acknowledgments

The editor and publishers would like to thank the following:

David Drummond, Chris Mason and the Mary Evans Picture Library for their help in researching the illustrations.

Derrick Witty the photographer.

Edmund Dulac, © Geraldine M. Anderson from *Stories from Hans Anderson*, Hodder and Stoughton.

Arthur Rackman from *Little Brother and Little Sister*, and *Fairy Tales of the Brothers Grimm*, Constable and Co., Ltd., by permission of Barbara Edwards.

The publishers have made every effort to trace copyright holders. If we have inadvertently omitted to acknowledge anyone we should be most grateful if this could be brought to our attention for correction at the earliest opportunity.